# GUNS FOR
# GENERAL WASHINGTON

# GUNS FOR GENERAL WASHINGTON

## A Story of the American Revolution

## SEYMOUR REIT

A TRUMPET CLUB SPECIAL EDITION

**Published by The Trumpet Club**
**1540 Broadway, New York, New York 10036**

ISBN 0-440-84610-2

This edition published by arrangement with
Harcourt Brace Jovanovich, Inc.
Map by Fiona King
Cover art by Richard Ross
Cover design by Martha Roach
Printed in the United States of America
January 1992

10 9 8 7 6 5 4 3 2
OPM

For Edmée

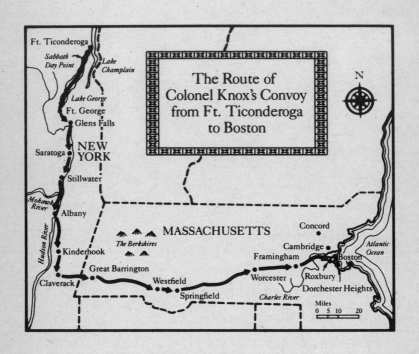

Ft. Ticonderoga
Sabbath Day Point
Lake Champlain
Lake George
Ft. George
Glens Falls

The Route of
Colonel Knox's Convoy
from Ft. Ticonderoga
to Boston

N

NEW YORK
Saratoga
Stillwater
Mohawk River
Albany

Hudson River

Kinderhook

The Berkshires
MASSACHUSETTS

Concord

Cambridge
Framingham
Boston
Atlantic Ocean

Great Barrington
Claverack
Westfield
Springfield
Worcester
Roxbury
Dorchester Heights
Charles River

Miles
0  5  10      20

# Contents

# About This Book

Paul Revere's midnight ride . . . Washington crossing the Delaware . . . the winter crisis at Valley Forge . . . Some events of America's War for Independence are known to us all. But there are other episodes, just as dramatic, that seem to have been lost in the dusty pages of history.

The subject of this book—the great cannon trek of 1775—is one of those remarkable events. It played a vital part in the early months of the revolution, but few people seem to know much about it. What you're about to read is factual and accurate. All the dates, times, and places are real. The people who took part in it are also real. And now, for the first time, the full account is being told.

Material for our drama came from many places. Colonel Henry Knox, the central player, kept a diary for part of the long journey. He also sent regular reports to General Washington. Another participant was a young boy named John P. Becker. Years later, in the 1830s, he wrote about his boyhood adventure for a newspaper called the *Albany Gazette*. The story was also mentioned in many histories, though not in detail.

This author is grateful for the accounts of historians who helped him to put the exciting pieces of the jigsaw puzzle together. Among those noted writers are Donald Barr Chidsey, North Callahan, Clay Perry, Howard H. Peckham, and Esther Forbes, author of a major biography of Paul Revere.

Others who deserve thanks for their kind help include William H. Hooks of Bank Street College; Harris Colt, proprietor of the Military Bookman in New York City; and Linda Russell, singer, musician, and authority on colonial songs and ballads. Thanks must also go to Margaret Peet for her excellent secretarial work.

Most of our country's history comes to us on printed pages. But there was a time before those pages were written, when people actually experienced the adventures we read about. To make past events truly come to life, the people involved must also come to life. We must really know how they felt and what they may have thought. To do this, the author has tried to "re-create" various speeches and thoughts for his characters. All of these inventive touches have been done with great care, in order to keep them true to the characters and true to their times.

As you read these pages, you may agree that Colonel Knox's great adventure was indeed a stirring, suspenseful, and important event in American history. It is a tale of courage and bravery—an episode that gave young America its first real victory, paving the way for the future of a great democratic nation.

From the east to the west
    blow the trumpet to arms;
Through the land let
    the sound of it flee;
Let the far and the near
    all unite with a cheer,
In defense of our Liberty Tree!

—Thomas Paine (1775)

# 1

# The Restless Rebel

*Crack! Crack! Crack!*

The sound of musket fire cut through the stillness of the sleeping camp. Colonial soldiers, bleary-eyed, tumbled out of their shelters with their weapons ready and raced toward the palisade. One of these men was a trooper named William Knox, who had been hoping to see action. Excited, he joined the others on the firing line and peered into the gray mist.

The news spread quickly among the waiting men. Hidden by morning fog, a British patrol had slipped across Mill Creek in an attempt to probe the rebel defenses. But an alert sentinel had spotted them in the marshes and opened fire. Others had joined in and the redcoats, giving up, had raced to their barge and escaped. The immediate crisis was over.

With shrugs and yawns, the soldiers trudged back to their warm beds. But Will Knox was too keyed up to go back to sleep. Unloading his musket, he walked across the drill grounds and climbed a rise called Prospect Hill. From here he could see his beloved Boston, locked in the hands of the enemy to the southeast. The city was only a few miles away, but it could well have been a thousand; the British had thrown a tight blockade around the city, and nobody could get in or out.

On this frosty morning in October of 1775, a sharp wind was blowing, but William was warmly dressed. Some weeks earlier a regiment of Pennsylvania frontiersmen had come marching into camp. Tough, hardy men, they wore long homespun shirts of butternut brown, fringed leather tunics, leggins, and Indian-style moccasins. Will had traded his best hunting knife, plus half a pound of sugar and some chewing tobacco, for a long shirt and tunic. He'd also fancied one of the fine coonskin caps worn by the Pennsylvania men, but those were scarce, so he had to make do with an ordinary militia tricorn.

Now, sitting with his back against a log rampart, the trooper studied the sweeping view. From where he sat the city looked like an island; it was entirely surrounded by water, except for a narrow causeway called Boston Neck. This strip of land was fortified and guarded by British redcoats. The rest of the area, lying in Boston Harbor, was patrolled by the powerful frigates of the Royal Navy.

Will had just turned nineteen and had joined the Continental Army after the fighting at Lexington and Concord. He'd been born in Boston on Sea Street and had lived there with his parents, brothers, and sisters. When Will was only three, his father had gone off to the West Indies to seek his fortune. He died while away and Will's older brother, Henry, became the head of the little family. Henry Knox was now twenty-five and a trusted officer on General Washington's staff. In Will's admiring eyes, Henry was a true

2

hero—at least, William felt, he *would* be a hero if there were only something to be heroic *about*.

Will Knox was half Irish and half Scottish—and both halves were hot-blooded. Like most volunteers, he was a solid patriot. Also an impatient one. He had come here to fight for liberty, eager for action and excitement. But the only action he'd found was trudging the countryside to collect firewood. And his only excitement was an occasional hunting trip to bring down some game for the regimental cook pot.

Restless and unhappy, William sat and chewed on a blade of spear grass. He raised his empty musket and idly aimed at a British frigate anchored off Dowe's Wharf. Slowly he moved his weapon, targeting the warships in the blockading fleet one by one. "In truth," he muttered to himself, "if this puny piece were a heavy cannon, I'd teach Bow-wow Howe and his lobsterbacks a thing or two. Aye, I'd send them packing . . ."

Behind him, Will heard the muffled roll of drums—a tattoo calling the troops to their morning drill. He stood up and started down the hill. The day had hardly begun, and already he felt weary. Wars, he knew, were *not* won by endless drilling. Why was he here? Why in blazes had he rushed to enlist? Why had he expected to find glory, when all he'd found so far was firewood?

As he hurried to join his company, Will Knox sighed with self-pity and boredom, unaware that an incredible adventure awaited him. The young soldier would soon be part of a strange expedition—one of the most daring and dangerous missions of the American Revolution.

# 2

## Stalemate in Boston

General Howe was in a bad mood. The cabin boy knew it because the tea things hadn't been touched, and when the general skipped his tea it meant a very bad mood indeed.

The young sailor picked up the silver tray and stood undecided. "Care for some fresh tea, sir? Nice 'n hot?"

"Get out," growled the general.

With a shrug the boy left, closing the door softly. Alone with his black thoughts, Major General Sir William Howe stared out the stern window of his cabin. Then he threw on a boat cloak, picked up his brass telescope, and stomped out on deck.

Howe stood at the rail and swept his glass back and forth across Boston Harbor. Five warships bristling with cannon stood in a half-circle around the city. His own ship, HMS *Somerset*, was a frigate of sixty-eight guns which served as the British command post. On the port side he saw the *Lively*, a twenty-gun sloop, and near her the brig *Glasgow*, mounting twenty-four guns. To starboard were the armed transports, *Cerberus* and *Symmetry*. Beyond them he could see the topmasts of the brig *Falcon*, guarding the mouth of the Charles River.

There were also a number of gun barges, armed schooners, and floating batteries at various key points. All of these formed a strong ring of oak and iron that held colonial Boston in a tight grip. With Howe's watchdogs on duty, not a single musket ball, not an ounce of gunpowder, not a morsel of bread or beef could get through to the weary, hungry Bostonians.

Howe lowered his brass telescope and snapped it shut. Yankee Doodle was locked up neatly, at least from the sea. But on the *land* side it was a different story—and the reason for Sir William's constant bad moods.

He narrowed his eyes and gazed toward the hills beyond Boston, half hidden in the cold November mist. Three miles away was the town of Cambridge. This was the site of Harvard College, founded years ago when the settlers were loyal to the King. Now the area was a fortified camp where the so-called "patriots" had their headquarters. Howe stomped along the deck, swearing under his breath. Patriots, indeed! They were nothing but traitors—a ragtag bunch of ignorant farmers, country bumpkins, riffraff, and ne'er-do-wells who had the colossal nerve to defy the laws of His Majesty, King George III.

Still, the general had to admit—albeit grudgingly—that these boors and roughnecks were surprisingly brave. They knew how to use their long muskets, pouring out volley after volley of deadly fire. The skirmishes at Lexington and Concord, the recent fighting at Breed's and Bunker hills, had proved that they could be tough and dangerous.

A staff officer stepped up to General Howe and touched his hat. "Word's come from our friends in Boston, sir. Three rebel regiments have just reached Cambridge. Militia from Pennsylvania, Virginia, and Maryland."

Sir William nodded and continued his pacing. Worse and worse. It wasn't just a Massachusetts affair anymore; the rebellion was spreading to *all* the colonies.

Cambridge was out of range of his heaviest guns— otherwise he'd blow the whole place to bits. He also had four thousand marines under his command—veterans whose fighting skills were famous. But this wasn't a big enough force to sweep across the Charles River and attack the Yanks in their stronghold. At Breed's Hill his redcoats had taken heavy casualties and many were out of action. There were just enough left to control Boston, protect the loyalists in the city, and fight off rebel patrols—and that was all.

The general had other problems. Scurvy, a dread disease, was increasing and fresh food was scarce. His hungry troops were living on biscuits and salt pork, half-rotted from lying so long in casks. The men had little to do except walk guard duty, drill on Boston Common, and go on scouting parties, hoping to round up a few cattle or sheep.

William Howe had been sent over to stamp out this colonial treachery. Instead he found himself in a stalemate. He knew from letters and messages that his expedition was becoming a laughingstock at home. One of the songs popular in England's pubs and taverns went:

> *In days of yore our noble troops*
> *Took warlike kings in battle.*
> *But now, alas, their valour fades—*
> *They capture harmless cattle!*

Back at the railing, Sir William watched a squad of redcoats climb down the rope ladder into a waiting barge.

Another party was going off to scour the countryside in search of food. They'd probably come back empty-handed.

He turned away, frowning. For the present he'd have to be patient and bide his time. But not for long. Heavy reinforcements were on their way from England; soon he'd have more ships, more guns, and a lot more troops. When these came he'd smash the rebels once and for all, and then sail home a hero. Yankee independence be hanged! Against the full force of England, the country bumpkins didn't stand a chance.

Feeling better at this happy thought, Sir William allowed himself a brief smile. As his bad mood slowly passed, he strode back to his cabin to order fresh tea.

# 3

# The New Commander

*Father and I went down to camp,*
*Along with Captain Gooding,*
*And there we saw the men and boys*
*As thick as hasty pudding.*

*Yankee Doodle keep it up,*
*Yankee Doodle dandy,*
*Mind the music and the step,*
*And with the girls be handy!*

A ragged squad, led by a lone fifer, made its noisy way through camp. The fife shrilled and squeaked, and the men raised their voices to follow the melody. The ditty had first been sung by the British to mock the rebels. But the colonists liked the lively tune, so they added new words and made it their own.

*There was Captain Washington*
*Upon a slapping stallion,*
*A-giving orders to his men;*
*I guess there were a million.*

*Yankee Doodle keep it up,*
*Yankee Doodle dandy,*
*Mind the music and the step,*
*And with the girls be handy!*

The squad, on its way to gather wood, marched past the camp headquarters. An officer working at his desk stopped to listen, and the song gave him a welcome lift. George Washington had been sitting and brooding. Like General Howe, his opponent aboard HMS *Somerset*, Washington was worried about the stalemate—but not for the same reasons.

Months earlier, in June of 1775, the Continental Congress had chosen him to command the new Continental Army. The delegates in Philadelphia couldn't have made a better choice. Tall, dignified, with good military experience, the Virginia landowner was a staunch patriot. When the call came, he accepted it gladly.

Full of exciting plans and high hopes, he had hurried to Massachusetts by fast coach. But after a few days in Cambridge, his excitement and hopes had begun to fade. What the general found when he reached headquarters was something close to chaos. The Continental Army was a force without shape; there was no organization and no discipline. Shelters were scattered everywhere, no two alike. The men were living in tumbledown shacks, rickety lean-tos, or tents patched together from scraps of canvas and blankets. Their clothes were shabby, and there were no uniforms except for a few companies funded by their wealthy officers.

Washington had a neat, precise military mind. Over and

over he tried to remember that his raw troops were colonists, not professional soldiers. They were a noisy, good-humored, democratic mob, willing and brave but *not* happy taking orders. In fact, orders and royal commands were the very things they were *against*. So they'd come together to put an end to King George's tyranny—this odd assortment of farmers and fishermen, carpenters and cobblers, tradesmen and teachers, barbers, blacksmiths, frontier scouts, seamen, clerks, weavers, tanners, tailors, shopkeepers, stonemasons, lumberjacks, and young men just seeking adventure. Also, the good pay of six dollars a month for army privates drew many colonials to the cause.

It was the easygoing disorder of his troops that troubled General Washington, but that could be corrected. These good-natured amateurs with their pitchforks and hunting rifles had to be welded into a real military force or the cause would be lost. Yes, rules and discipline had to be established. Officers had to dress according to rank, and their orders had to be carried out. March and drill practice would be increased. Work parties would be organized. Sanitation would be improved.

Washington had wanted to make soldiers of his men—and under his leadership the changes came quickly. Still, many problems remained, and the commander wasn't sure they could *ever* be solved.

For one thing, all the discipline in the world couldn't combat the weather. Winter was coming and soon it would turn bitterly cold. There were thousands of troops in Cambridge, badly dressed and poorly housed. The countryside had been stripped bare, and firewood was scarce. The army was short of blankets, soap, shoes, medical supplies, tools, muskets, and gunpowder. In August, Washington had been told that the arsenal held over three hundred barrels of gunpowder. Later, when these figures were checked, it turned out that only *ninety* barrels were on hand; which meant that each man could fire his musket eight or nine times before the powder would be gone!

What troubled the general even more was that he had no artillery. Several big siege guns, hidden in Concord, had been captured by the redcoats. Now there were only a few small brass cannons that could fire six-pound shots. Compared to Howe's weapons, they were no better than popguns.

Sitting at his desk on a cold November day, General Washington worried about all this. Outwardly he seemed calm, but his spirits were low. Picking up his quill pen, he continued the letter he'd begun to his friend Joseph Reed in Philadelphia. In it he wrote: "Could I have foreseen what I have, and am like to experience, no consideration on earth would have induced me to accept this command."

The general put down his pen, sealed the letter, and buttoned his coat. He stepped outside. From the top of Prospect Hill—the very spot where Will Knox had stood earlier—he could see Boston clearly. With his pocket telescope he could make out the red jackets of Howe's marines drilling on the Common and patrolling Barton's Point.

Like his British enemy, Washington needed a victory. On the land side the rebels were in control, surrounding Boston in a huge ring from Roxbury to Chelsea on the Mystick River. In manpower they far outnumbered the British. But the British had all the gunpowder and all the artillery. If the patriots tried to drive them from Boston Harbor, Howe's warships could bombard the city. Or by firing "carcasses"—thin shells filled with flaming oily rags—they could burn it to the ground. The forces were deadlocked. Without cannons the colonists couldn't liberate Boston. Without men the British couldn't attack Cambridge.

Both sides had spies in Boston, and Washington knew

that Howe was expecting reinforcements. Meanwhile, winter was here and smallpox was creeping through the big camp. Some of the volunteers, sick, bored, and lonesome for their families, were beginning to drift away. When the icy winds came, with no victories to raise morale, the trickle of deserters would become a flood. Washington was afraid that his army, short of so many things, might fall apart—and with it the whole precious cause.

> *I can't tell you half I saw,*
> *They kept up such a smother;*
> *So I tipped my hat, made a bow,*
> *And scampered home to mother.*

> *Yankee Doodle keep it up,*
> *Yankee Doodle dandy,*
> *Mind the music and the step,*
> *And with the girls be handy!*

The squad, with its lone fifer, came straggling back to camp. Their cart held very little wood, since every tree, fence, and barn-siding for miles around had already been fed to the campfires.

Slowly the general walked back to his quarters. At the rate the army used it, firewood would soon be worth more than gold. Of course the men needed fuel to stay warm, but they also needed the fuel of success. His ragged soldiers needed a victory. Time was running out. Somehow the Continental Army had to work a miracle; if they could defeat Howe and set Boston free, it would electrify the colonies. That would put heart into the rebellion before it was too late.

Or was it too late already? General Washington wasn't sure.

# 4

# Paul and William

"You, boy! Come here!" The marine raised his musket suspiciously.

Paul turned and saw the redcoat. Quick as a hare, he vaulted a low wall and raced into a nearby alley. The soldier's heavy boots came pounding after him, but fifteen-year-old Paul Revere, Jr., knew the back routes and byways of Boston far better than any lobsterback. He had spent all afternoon fishing in Mill Cove and had been lucky enough to land two plump fish—and he wasn't about to let some British bully take them away.

Hanging on to his precious catch, Paul turned a bend in the alley, dove through a hedge, and raced along a ditch. He cut to a weedy path behind Friends Street, circled Cockerel Church, and darted across Middle Street. From there another alley took him to North Square, where he stopped to catch his breath. The marine had long since given up the chase, and Paul was able to cross the square and slip into the Revere house by the back way.

He bolted the door, dropped his catch onto the kitchen table, and leaned his pole against the wall. Now he'd have a good dinner—but first there was something to attend to. He put one fish in a skillet. The other, he wrapped in a scrap of paper and tucked inside his patched coat. He looked out the parlor window to make sure the coast was clear, then hurried to Clark's Wharf.

As far back as Paul could remember, his father had kept a workshop here on the wharf. In the old days, before the troubles, Mr. Revere had been Boston's most successful craftsman. His workshop turned out beautiful silver pitchers, bowls, and tankards. He created surgeons' tools, copper engravings, serving spoons, eyeglass frames, church Communion cups, handsome sword hilts, even silver dog collars. And as a sideline, busy Mr. Revere acted as a dentist, pulling bad teeth or making false ones of ivory and gold wire.

Now, with his father branded a "traitor" by the British, the shop had been left in charge of a silversmith named Isaac Clemens. Since old Clemens was a Tory, loyal to the king, the redcoats had left the shop alone. Paul Junior didn't like Mr. Clemens much (he didn't like *anyone* opposed to the cause), but the man was important to the family, so the boy thought a gift of food a good idea. In Boston that winter, Tories got just as hungry as patriots.

The gift was appreciated and Clemens thanked Paul warmly. "Your father and I," the old man added, "don't agree on much these days. But I grant you, son, he's the best craftsman in the colonies. Send word to him, if you can, that old Clem is keeping a keen eye on everything."

Back home Paul fried his supper with the last of the stovewood and ate it slowly. There were no sounds in the empty house. And none outside, except for the whining of a hungry dog and the pounding of boots as a squad of soldiers marched by.

Sitting there, Paul Junior decided that being lonely was the worst of all feelings. Even worse than being afraid. Under the hard thumb of the British, Boston was a town of ghosts and memories—shadow images that filled his thoughts and empty hours. As he cleaned up after his little meal, Paul remembered the good times before the warships came. North Square, where the Reveres lived, had been a bustling area ringed with neat, prosperous houses. There were handsome trees, tidy gardens, shiny brass nameplates, elegant doorways, and fancy hitching-posts for horses and carriages. And at the far end of the square was Old North Church, one of the finest in all New England.

Three times a week the square had become a grand town market where food of all kinds could be bought. Paul remembered the stalls piled with fruits and farm vegetables, fat sacks of grain, and firkins of churned butter. Other booths held turkeys, hams, mutton, and veal. There were quails and partridges. There were bags of flour and rye meal, kegs of oysters, tubs of pickled pork. There were venison and bear steaks brought in by hunters. And lobsters were plentiful, too, at a halfpenny each.

Now it was all changed. The stalls were gone—and so were most of the people who once brought life and excitement to Paul's world. His father had helped to rouse the countryside at Lexington and Concord; now he was hiding in Philadelphia and working with John Hancock, Sam Adams, and the other colonial leaders. His mother, sisters, and brothers had also fled, slipping away in a horse-drawn cart in the middle of the night. Only Paul remained at home—and for a reason. Many supporters of the rebellion had left everything behind when they escaped from Boston.

To keep discipline, General Howe had decreed martial law: thousands of people still lived in the besieged city, and the marines had strict orders not to harm them. But empty, abandoned houses were looked upon as fair game. The redcoats had looted these quickly, taking everything of value. They'd even ripped out doors, stairways, fine wood panels, and hand-carved railings to feed their campfires.

The destruction was ongoing. Recently, the steeple of West Street Church had been pulled down for fuel. In Old South Church the pews had been torn out and gravel spread over the floor—now it served as a riding ring for General Burgoyne's fancy horses. Only one pew had been left in the church—and it had been turned into a pigsty.

Because Paul still lived in the house, the Revere family home had been spared by the redcoats. But he felt their hatred and contempt. Now, sitting on his bed, the boy took a crumpled, stained piece of paper from his shirt pocket. It was a letter from his father that had been smuggled to him, and Paul had read it over and over. In an artist's fine hand, Paul Senior had written:

My Son: It is now in your power to be of service to me, your mother, and yourself. I beg you to keep yourself safely at home. Behave well. Attend to my business. Do not come away until I send you word.

Your loving father, P. R.

Paul slipped the letter back into his pocket and frowned. He was dying to leave and join the rebels in Cambridge. He was old enough—*almost*—to be with the Continental Army and fight beside the other men. But he knew that was impossible. He'd made a solemn promise to stay; it was now his responsibility. In a way he was like a soldier under orders—a soldier whose enemies were fear and loneliness.

Unable to sleep, Paul paced the floor of his room. *Plague take General William Howe! Plague take his warships! Plague take his cannons and his redcoats and—*

TAP, TAP . . . tap-tap-tap . . .

Startled by the signal, he raced downstairs to the kitchen. Through the window he could see Will Knox's face, pale in the darkness. Quickly, Paul unlatched the back door and pulled his friend inside.

William, tall and gangly, wiped his nose and grinned. "Greetings from General Washington and the Sons of Liberty, Paulie."

At nineteen, William was four years older than Paul Junior, but they'd been friends for a long time. Together, as boys, they'd gone swimming off Hudson's Point and fishing in Mill Pond. They'd explored the byways of the city and played at ninepins on Boston Common. Paul was delighted to see Will again.

"How'd you get here?" he asked.

"Toby rowed me over. It was simple. No moon tonight; it's black as pitch. So I decided to pay you a visit and see how things were going in Boston."

Paul shook his head anxiously. "You dasn't do this, Will. It's way too dangerous. If they catch you they'll put you in chains for sure. Or—or worse."

William grinned again and held up a fat, fresh-killed rabbit. "Lobsterbacks don't scare me. Look, I fetched you a present. Shot it this afternoon near Phipps Farm."

Paul took the rabbit happily. "Well now, I do thank you. I'll have rabbit stew for supper tomorrow. But I still think you should—"

His friend waved a carefree hand, kicked off his boots, and sat down near the stove, still a bit warm from Paul's cooking. "Lordy," he sighed, "this feels good. It's powerful cold in Cambridge, and barely any firewood left. Not enough to warm a man's big toe."

Paul pulled a stool up next to his friend, and stared at him with envy. William was a Massachusetts soldier and his older brother, Henry, was a colonel of artillery on Washington's staff. They were *really* in the fight—not sitting it out in Boston like he was.

"Things are bad here," Paul said sadly, "and getting worse. What's happening, Will? When's Washington going to come and throw them out?"

William shrugged. "We're trapped, Paulie. Scotched and hog-tied. We've almost no powder and ball left. And we can't make a move without cannons. If we marched on Boston, Howe would blow the whole city to bits, and us along with it."

Paul looked thoughtful. "Any news of my father?"

His visitor nodded. "He's been riding express for the congress. And I hear tell he's etching some new copper plates. The delegates want to print money—our *own* currency instead of the king's paper. New currency for a new country."

Paul frowned. "It's a grand gesture, but we need a lot more than that. They say Howe's getting reinforcements. If we don't stop him, there won't *be* a new country."

Will got up and drank water from a tin dipper at the kitchen pump. He had an odd, eager look on his weathered face. "Paulie, I'm not right sure yet, but I'll pass you a secret. Not a word to anyone, mind you, but something big is brewing. My brother, Henry, has a marvelous plan. Some of the officers think he's daft, but Henry doesn't care. He's going to talk to the War Council tomorrow."

"What's it about?"

William pulled on his boots. "Can't say—I've said too

much already. But pray hard that the council lets him go ahead. And now, I'd best be on my way."

The young trooper gave his friend a clumsy bear hug. Then, with a quick salute, he slipped out the door and melted into the night.

Paul hung the rabbit in the wash shed and climbed the stairs. Will's visit had cheered him up. He didn't feel quite so lonely anymore; he decided to get ready for bed.

Lying there, staring at the ceiling, Paul thought about Colonel Knox. What was this "marvelous plan" Will had mentioned? And why did some of the officers think Henry Knox was daft? Well, no matter. Daft or sane, he would pray for the colonel. He would pray hard.

In the distance he could hear the thud of marching boots. The British were changing the guard company at the North Battery. The ominous sound gradually faded, and in the cold, dark silence Paul dozed off, wondering about tomorrow.

# 5

## "Go Ahead, Henry . . ."

The day after Will's secret visit, the War Council met in Cambridge. The council was made up of leading officers of the army; among them was Henry Knox.

Everyone at headquarters, including the commander, liked Colonel Knox. He was only twenty-five, but he had a way about him that inspired confidence. Over six feet tall with big shoulders and a booming laugh, he was lively, enthusiastic, and completely fearless. In fact, some of the men thought Henry wanted to take on the British all by himself and lick them single-handedly.

Before the rebellion, Henry had owned a bookshop on Boston's Cornhill Street and Will had worked with him. It was an unusual shop; along with books, they sold tobacco, musical instruments, telescopes, patent medicines, and a brand of snuff said to "cure deafness and improve memory." But the books were Henry's main interest, and he read most of them. Especially the ones dealing with weapons and warfare. Between his reading and his long talks with army men, Henry had become something of an expert on artillery. His shop had also been a meeting-place for Boston's Whigs—the party that wanted independence for the colonies. Samuel Adams, John Hancock, Nathaniel Greene, Paul Revere, and others all met at Henry's to gossip, talk politics, and grumble about the stupidity of the British.

But Henry liked action as well as talk, so he became a lieutenant in a militia company called the Grenadier Corps. At that time the British were closing in on "rebel troublemakers" and he was ordered not to leave the city without permission. Henry was now in great danger, so he and his wife, Lucy, decided to escape. Late at night (like many others) they slipped away from the city, leaving everything behind. Everything but Henry's handsome militia sword, which Mrs. Knox managed to hide under her ample petticoats.

Once Lucy was safe in the town of Worcester, Henry hurried to join the colonial army. His knowledge and experience were badly needed, and before long he was made colonel of artillery. Of course it was just the right job for him and he was delighted. But when he asked at headquarters where the artillery was kept, a young officer replied sheepishly, "Uh, well—I'm afraid, sir, there *isn't* any."

Colonel Knox was shocked. And alarmed. And very angry. What good was an artillery colonel without artillery? And what good was an army without heavy weapons? If *this* army didn't have cannons, he'd jolly well *find* some.

Henry worried about the problem. He studied his maps and talked to the experts at headquarters. At last he came up with a wild plan that brought him to Washington's War Council. And now these high officers were ready to hear what young Knox had in mind.

While the men gathered around, Henry unrolled a large map that showed the colonies of New York, New Hampshire, and Massachusetts. In northern New York, between two lakes, there was a black dot marked *Fort Ticonderoga*. Henry jabbed his finger at the dot. "Gentlemen," he announced. "Here are the guns we need."

The officers looked at him, a bit puzzled. They all knew about Fort Ticonderoga. Years earlier, during the French and Indian wars, this outpost had been seized by the British. They'd stayed in control until May of 1775, when Benedict Arnold, Ethan Allen, and Allen's "Green Mountain Boys" captured it in a surprise attack. Now the huge fort was in the hands of the rebels, but it was far from any fighting areas.

Colonel Knox read from a slip of paper. "According to Captain Arnold," he said, "they found a lot of heavy artillery when they took Ticonderoga. There were one hundred eighty-three cannons, nineteen mortars, three howitzers, and fifty-one swivel guns—plus barrels of flints and crates of musket balls. Some of the big pieces may be in good condition. I propose, sirs, to go to the fort and bring them here to Cambridge."

A few of the officers frowned. Others just shook their heads in puzzlement. One old general growled, "How do you plan to do it, colonel? Will you fit your cannons with wings and fly them here?"

The others laughed, but Henry stood his ground. "Wings won't be necessary, sir. Give me a dozen men and authority to hire more if I have to, and we'll handle it."

A major of infantry swept his hand over the map. "This is bad terrain, Knox. You're talking about three hundred miles of mountain wilderness. No roads, no bridges, hardly any footpaths. How the devil are you going to move heavy guns?"

"I'll use everything," Henry answered. "Boats, barges, sleds, ox teams. Whatever I can build, borrow, or buy. All I need are funds and men."

"What about the weather?" someone asked. "This time of year you'll have ice storms, blizzards, heavy snow. Everything will freeze solid. You'll *never* get through."

The others nodded in agreement. They turned away and began muttering to each other. Henry caught words like "impractical," "absurd," and "foolhardy." The old general spoke up again. "I admire your spirit, Knox, but the whole thing's impossible. Waste of time and good money. It simply can't be done."

Henry sensed the mood of the group and his hopes began to fade. He hadn't convinced them; his wonderful scheme was about to be rejected. But at that point General Washington turned to him, put a fatherly hand on his arm, and said, "They may well be right. Considering the odds, it *does* sound impossible. But we need those guns and if anyone can get them, *you* can. So go ahead, Henry. Go ahead and try."

An hour later, Henry Knox burst into his brother's tent. William, sitting on his cot, was trying to sew a button onto his tunic. He looked up, saw his brother's face, and let out a whoop. "They accepted the plan!"

Henry sat down, beaming. "Right, lad. At least Washington did—and that's what matters. Official permission has to come from Philadelphia, but that's only a formality. The general wants us to get started, and we're to spare no trouble or expense. He's rushing a letter to General Schuyler in Albany, ordering him to give us all the help we need."

William narrowed his eyes and smiled. "You said 'we' and 'us.' That means I get to go with you?"

His brother laughed. "I have no choice; I promised father

before he left for the Indies that I'd always keep an eye on you. So finish that button—we've got a lot of work to do."

One of the ferrymen on the Charles River was William's friend, a grizzled veteran known as Old Toby. Early that evening, Toby tapped on the kitchen window of the Revere house in Boston. When Paul Junior answered, he handed him a note, winked, and hobbled away. Paul opened the scrawled note and read:

Paulie, The plan is under way. I won't be seeing you for a spell. Keep praying.

—W. K.

# 6

# To Ticonderoga

On November 28, 1775, Henry and Will Knox left camp on horseback, leading a pack mule loaded with supplies for their journey.

Ahead lay miles of wilderness, craggy mountain ranges, ice-clogged rivers, deep gorges, and valleys thick with stands of birch, spruce, and white pine. The woods were teeming with beavers, deer, black bears, and other animals, but there were few people. On their way the travelers would be isolated, except for a few river towns and a scattering of Iroquois Indians living in bark-covered longhouses.

Their first goal was the city of Albany. But before that, they stopped at Worcester so Henry could say good-bye to Lucy. William, staying tactfully out of the way, watched the couple sympathetically. They kept up a brave front, but Will saw anxiety in Lucy's face. They didn't put it into words, but all three knew that the mission was dangerous. Anything could happen. If there were a bad accident, if they were ambushed by Indians or by the British, husband and wife might never see each other again.

Soon Henry and Will swung into their saddles to continue west. Lucy stood at the door, her eyes fixed on her big, brawny husband. As the men clattered down the icy road, the mule trotting behind, her smile faded. She raised a hand and whispered softly, "Take care, my dear. Take care . . ."

The weather turned colder and the wind rose. Muffled in scarves and heavy coats, the brothers rode past Webb Hill, forded the Connecticut River, and came to the village of Pittsfield. Here they crossed the border into New York State, turned north, and reached Albany on the first of December.

General Philip Schuyler, commanding the Albany garrison, had already been alerted by Washington. Like the others, Schuyler thought it was a fool's errand and that Knox's plan was impossible. But he was a soldier under orders, and he gave the travelers all the help he could. While there, Henry studied his maps and arranged for the building of sturdy carts and sleds. When these were ready, they would be rushed north.

Two days later, the men left Albany and headed toward their final goal. Fort Ticonderoga was at the northern tip of a huge body of water called Lake George. Beyond this was another big lake called Lake Champlain. The French had built their fort between these lakes so they could control both waterways. First it was called Fort Carillon, but when the British had seized it they gave it an Indian name, *Ti-conderoga*. Early in 1775, with the country in rebellion, the fort was attacked again. Now it was in the hands of the colonists. Benedict Arnold, who had helped capture the outpost, reported that it was filled with cannons—weapons hauled there over many years, first by French troops and later by the British.

Riding beside his brother, William felt his excitement building. He could hardly believe his good fortune. Only a few weeks ago he'd been bored and unhappy, afraid that the war would pass him by. Now here he was on a vital mission, under secret orders from General Washington himself!

Turning toward Henry, Will noticed him frowning. Something was on his brother's mind and Will was curious. "Do you think," he asked, "that Captain Arnold's report is really reliable?"

The big man shrugged. "He said there were close to two hundred guns, and I don't doubt the count is right. But that doesn't mean they're *usable*, Will. Guns aren't any use if they're pitted and rusted—or if they were deliberately spiked by the British. We may be in for a disappointment, but there's no sense worrying. Good or bad, we'll know soon enough."

For three days the brothers rode north through the woodlands, cooking over small campfires and sleeping under the frosty stars. On December fourth they reached Fort George at the lower end of the lake. They stayed overnight to rest, and Henry took this opportunity to write letters—one an official report to George Washington, the other a note to Lucy. He told her again how much he loved her and closed by confessing, "I think of you continually."

Next day the two men sailed up the full length of Lake George. Will stared ahead, alive with anticipation—and there was Ticonderoga at last. The old fort was held by militia from nearby towns, and the commander had been told to give Colonel Knox all the men and supplies he needed. The travelers were overjoyed to reach their goal—

and even more excited to find hundreds of cannons inside the fort.

"Arnold was right!" Henry exulted. "Look at them all—enough artillery here for ten armies!" Along the high fortress walls and in the huge arsenal, they found weapons of every shape and size: iron cannons and brass cannons, mobile guns on wheels and fixed guns bolted to wooden frames, heavy fat mortars and small bronze ones called "cohorns." Some of the cannons had stubby barrels only twelve inches in length. Others were great iron brutes eleven feet long and weighing two tons each. Colonel Knox also found, to his joy and relief, that some of the weapons were in very good shape.

Their next job was to choose a team. "We'll take volunteers only," Henry told Will, "but no clerks or city lads. We want roughnecks, the rougher the better. Mountain men, hunters, lumberjacks—fellows used to hard living. We'll have our share of work before we see Cambridge again."

Will was put in charge of assembling boats. These would ferry the prizes down the lake to the waiting carts. On Lake George there were three main kinds of boats: flat-bottomed barges, or "scows"; wide-beamed shallow vessels known as "bateaux"; and small, fast sailboats called "piraguas." The barges and bateaux, fitted with sails, would carry the heavy cargo. The frisky piraguas were just right for scouting and communication.

Three hectic days flew by as men were chosen, boats fitted out, and cannons dragged down to the Ticonderoga dock. Henry, carrying his scribbled notes, went over the list with the fort commander. "We're taking fifty-nine pieces, altogether," he said. "Thirty iron cannons, thirteen of brass, and sixteen mixed guns—mortars, howitzers, and cohorns." The cargo also included a large barrel of thirty thousand flints and twenty-three boxes of lead bars. The flints were for the army's flintlock muskets, and the lead would be melted down for bullets.

Soon every box, barrel, and cannon was ready for the boats. Hurrying along the dock as the loading began, the brothers looked at each other with tense faces. They had been much too busy to think; now it was as if they suddenly realized what lay ahead. They were about to move sixty tons of metal cargo through the cruelest weeks of winter, across three hundred miles of wild country—a dangerous, rugged trip people told them could not be done.

William wiped his nose and tried hard to smile. Henry cleared his throat and slowly scratched his chin. Then he roused himself, grinned, and patted Will on the shoulder. "No turning back now, little brother, so let's get started. We've a fair way to go—and the general is waiting."

# 7

# Trouble on the Lake

Loading the flat-bottoms took time. First, each gun had to be dismantled, then the heavy parts had to be lashed together. The loaders also had to carefully balance the weight in each vessel. Henry's team was just what he wanted—a group of tough, muscular men who were used to hardship and danger. He had also hired some local boatmen who knew the lake well.

By midafternoon on December ninth everything was loaded. At last the sails were raised and they started south. William rode in the first barge, the others following behind. For himself, Henry chose a fast piragua with a good pilot, so he could range up and down among the moving vessels.

Groaning under their loads, the boats crept through the gray water while Will nervously tested the wind. Luckily it was strong, whipping briskly from the northeast and filling the little sails. Even with their loads the boats moved steadily, and Henry hoped to make the thirty-three-mile voyage in just a few days. November had been a terribly cold month and thick ice had formed on both shores of the lake. Here and there, big jagged ice chunks were piled up like miniature white mountains. But there was an open channel right down the center.

Watching with sharp eyes, Will guided the flotilla through this middle passage. He was flattered that Henry had picked him to lead the way, but he was nervous as well. It was a big responsibility; also, some of the men were a good bit older than he was and might resent taking his orders.

As dusk closed in, Henry decided to find a place to stop for the night. Leaving the boats, he sailed on ahead. Suddenly he heard a splintery crash and muffled shouts!

Henry turned the piragua and raced back to the convoy. "What happened?" he shouted.

"It's my fault!" his brother wailed. "Blast me for my fool carelessness!"

In the growing darkness, Will had begun to daydream. He'd allowed his barge to drift and it had run aground on hidden rocks. The damage wasn't serious, but the barge was leaking and would need repairs. Two bateaux came alongside and cargo was shifted from the damaged scow. Several men, daring the frigid water, went over the side onto the rocks and managed to shove the boat free. Henry's pilot led the convoy to a sheltered cove called Sabbath Day Point. Luckily it was fairly free of ice. The men ran the leaky barge up on shore, and the others dropped anchor nearby.

Fires were quickly built so the ones who'd gone overboard could get warm and dry their clothes. Meanwhile carpenters patched the damaged bow with tar and lumber brought from the fort. The barge was pushed back into the water for a test. Will breathed a long sigh of relief when it proved seaworthy.

31

By now everyone was exhausted, so Colonel Knox decided to stay put until morning. Canvas bags of biscuits and dried salt meat were brought ashore. Huddled around the campfires, the men settled down to a cold, uncomfortable night.

Suddenly a group of strange painted faces loomed from the surrounding bushes.

"Injuns!" somebody shouted.

The men jumped up and scrambled for knives and muskets, ready for a fight. But it proved a false alarm. A band of Algonquins living nearby were curious about all the activity. They had come to investigate, bringing a gift with them—a big haunch of roast venison. It made a fine and unexpected meal for the tired travelers.

At dawn they broke camp and the convoy set off again. Henry was worried about arrangements at the southern end of the lake. "Schuyler's supposed to have carts and oxen for us, but I don't want to take chances or lose any more time," he said to his brother. "I'll move ahead and meet you at Fort George."

In his fast boat Henry reached the fort without trouble. He found preparations under way. But William and the convoy were not so lucky. Wind currents on mountain lakes could be tricky and unpredictable. For a while the wind had been their friend, but it began to fade. Then it picked up again—blowing hard in the opposite direction. Now they faced a problem: the bateaux were too clumsy and heavy to work against a head wind in the narrow channel.

Will stood up and faced the barges behind him. "Take in your sails and break out the sweeps!" he bellowed. "We'll have to row!"

Holes had been cut on the sides of each boat in case oars, or "sweeps," were needed. On each vessel, the crews put the oars in place, then began to pull.

It was hard, back-breaking work, but William set the pace and the men rowed steadily. Together they fought the sly wind that threatened to blow them all the way back to Ticonderoga. It had been slow going before, but now their progress was even slower.

Meanwhile Colonel Knox, waiting at Fort George, was in a fever of uncertainty. A whole day passed while he walked the windswept shore, anxious to know what was happening. Finally he sent a rider on a fast horse up the side of the lake to investigate.

After several hours the rider returned. His horse was winded and his clothes spattered with icy mud. He reported that there had been another accident. A second barge had sprung a leak and started to go down, but the men were able to shift the cargo before the barge sank. "The boats are moving again," the rider said, "and they've only ten more miles to go." Henry was thankful for the news but knew he wouldn't relax until every man and gun was ashore.

Then, on the morning of the fifteenth, six days after they'd started, a thick fog drifted across the southern end of Lake George. The fog added to Henry's worries; he could do nothing but wait. He peered and paced and tried to stay calm. Where were the boats? Was Will safe? Had there been another accident? What if the guns wound up at the bottom of the lake? He stared into the fog, his fears growing. Maybe the council officers were right, after all. Maybe he really was doomed to fail.

The colonel groaned to himself. Had he made a blunder? Was the whole plan unrealistic—just a vain and foolish dream?

The fog blanketed the shore. Filled with guilt and worry, Colonel Knox continued to pace back and forth, back and forth. The hours ticked by. Still no sign of the convoy. Henry felt miserable. His daring plan was falling apart. He'd have to go back to Cambridge in disgrace . . .

Suddenly he froze. Was he imagining things? No, there it was again—a faint voice singing in the fog!

> *We had a little ship*
> *and she sailed upon the sea,*
> *And the name of that ship*
> *was the Golden Vanity . . .*

The colonel held his breath and listened hard. He began to smile as he heard the voice again:

> *And we thought she would be taken*
> *by the Spanish enemy,*
> *As she sailed upon the lowland,*
> *lowland low,*
> *Sailed upon the lowland sea!*

Henry squinted through the gloom. A ghostly line of boats was creeping toward shore. He watched the oars rise and fall, rise and fall, as the convoy drew closer. The lead barge was listing badly, but he could see Will standing in the bow, baling water and singing in a loud tenor voice.

One by one, the barges scraped up on the pebbly slope. As the weary men collapsed over their oars, William climbed ashore and came toward his brother. His face was haggard and there were dark circles under his eyes. With a big grin, he gave Henry a fancy salute and said, "Ticonderoga Navy, sir—reporting as ordered."

At that moment, Colonel Knox had never felt happier.

# 8

# The Colonel Reports

With the guns safely at Fort George, the next move was to
start overland. The pilots who had volunteered for the lake
passage were paid, thanked, and sent home. The brothers
added a group of men who knew how to handle horses and
oxen, and a platoon of soldiers was assigned to the convoy.

General Schuyler had kept his word: many carts and sleds
had been sent from Albany, and more were on the way.
The sleds were made of thick wooden planks, and the
wooden runners were reinforced with iron strips. Some colonists also came to the fort to offer their own sturdy wagons.

One of these was a farmer named Becker who brought
his twelve-year-old son, John, with him. John—known as
J. P.—had begged for the chance to go with his pa, and he
became the youngest member of Colonel Knox's team.
Becker had signed on for the run to Springfield, Massachusetts—a distance of several hundred miles—and he and
J. P. were put in charge of a big brass nine-pounder. It was

called that because it could fire a cannonball weighing approximately nine pounds. Four strong horses were used to haul this gun on Becker's wagon. But the heaviest weapons—the eighteen-pounders and twenty-four-pounders—needed the pulling power of eight oxen, yoked in pairs.

The scene at the lakefront was chaotic, but there was order in the confusion. J. P., wide-eyed, watched in excitement as the men hoisted cannons onto the sleds, rolled carts into line, studied maps, bridled horses, loaded tools and supplies, and hitched oxen to vehicles. Through it all, Henry and Will were everywhere, shouting orders, helping to load, and keeping an eye on their precious cargo.

It wasn't until the next day that Henry could sit down and write to General Washington. His quill pen raced over the paper as he explained that the guns had finally reached Fort George. Then he went on:

It is not easy to conceive the difficulties we had transporting them across the lake, owing to the advanced season of the year and contrary winds; but the danger is now past. Three days ago it was uncertain whether we could have gotten them until next spring but now, thanks be to God, we can go forward. I have had made 42 exceeding strong sleds, and have provided 80 yoke of oxen to drag them as far as Springfield, where I shall get fresh animals to carry them to camp. I expect to move on to Saratoga on Wednesday or Thursday next, trusting that between now and then we shall have a fine fall of snow, which will enable us to proceed further and make the carriage easy. If that shall be the case, I hope in sixteen or seventeen days' time to be able to present to your Excellency a noble train of artillery.

Henry sealed the note and handed it to a rider who had been standing by. He stepped outside for a last-minute check. Everything was in order. In a little while the journey would begin.

As he finished his inspection, William fell in beside him. The brothers nodded to each other without exchanging any words, for there was nothing more to say. The lake trip had been dangerous, but it was behind them. Now, they hoped, the convoy's worst troubles were over.

# 9

# News and Rumors

Somewhere across town, church bells began to ring. Finishing his breakfast of biscuits and cheese, Paul listened. That would be King's Chapel, he decided, over on Treamount Street. Probably a funeral for another smallpox victim. These days the bells tolled often for the dead. The pox was everywhere, striking people without regard for their politics or for history. Tory and Whig, royalist and neutral—everyone was fair game for the deadly sickness.

*Gone away*, moaned the church bells. *Gone away . . . gone away . . .*

Paul gathered the leftovers of his breakfast and put them in a tin box. Nobody in Boston wasted a single bit of food, no matter how small it might be.

*Farewell*, cried the bells. *Farewell . . . farewell . . .*

In the old days, Paul thought, church bells had sounded different. He had loved to hear them calling across the rooftops. Even on sad occasions they rang out strongly, serenely, full of life and hope. Now, it seemed, they were always dull and gloomy, as if mourning for a dying city.

Paul pulled on a jacket, grabbed his cap, and slipped out of the house, locking the door behind him. Crossing Fish Street, he passed a company of redcoats standing at rest. Their muskets slanted carelessly every which way. Sullen and bored, they glared at Paul with cold eyes. The boy looked the other way and tried to appear small and unimportant. He hated the British for making him feel weak and fearful—and despised himself for giving in to those feelings.

*Take care*, warned the bells. *Take care . . . take care . . .*

He walked quickly past Faneuil Hall, once the main public market and now a barracks for Howe's marines. Partway down Merchant's Row he turned and walked out on Long Wharf. This great pier, stretching two thousand feet into Boston Harbor, was a wonder of engineering admired all over the colonies. Once it had been a busy meeting place, the center of Boston's shipping trade. Here, in earlier days, contracts were signed and precious cargoes bought and sold. Along the north side of the wharf were warehouses, shops, and business offices. The south side of the pier had been left free for the docking of sailing ships. Even at low tide, the wharf could handle the biggest schooners on the Atlantic Ocean.

Today, as usual, the berths were unused, except for a small cutter flying the British flag. The shops and offices were dark and empty. Some of them had been boarded up for safety, but the planks had been torn off long ago and used for fuel—and so had the furniture inside.

Here and there on the pier, Paul saw small groups of people, their faces worn and their clothes shabby. With Boston trapped in Howe's blockade, citizens often gathered on the wharf to hear the latest news and rumors. Paul moved among the different groups, searching for a face. His eyes brightened. Near the south end of the pier, he spotted Old Toby sitting against a wooden piling, holding a fishing pole.

When Toby showed up on Long Wharf it usually meant interesting gossip. Paul strolled over and sat next to the boatman, his long legs hanging over the platform. Without turning his head, Toby touched his battered, shapeless hat. The hat had once belonged to a ship's captain, and since Toby was a man of the sea, he felt entitled to wear it. "Morning to you, Master Paul."

Paul nodded. "Morning to you, Toby. How are you faring?"

Toby made a face. "Well enough, thankee. Except for an empty belly."

"You might have some luck with your fishing," Paul said.

The old boatman shrugged. "I've got a powerful fat worm on my hook. Mayhap I'll catch a bit, if the redcoats haven't fished the harbor clean."

They sat for a while side by side, and Paul waited patiently. When Toby had news he would share it in his own way, in his own good time. He moved the pole about in the water, then cleared his throat. "Did you ever hear tell of a Captain John Manly?"

Paul nodded, curious. "A privateer, isn't he? Licensed by the council to go after British vessels?"

Toby grunted. "Aye, that be he. Commands an armed brig called the *Lee*. Word's come that he captured a British supply ship, the *Nancy*, out on Boston Bay. Took the ship, put a prize crew aboard, and sailed 'er into Cape Ann. Washington's sending four companies to get the cargo and carry it down to Cambridge."

"Were there good pickings?" Paul asked.

"The best, lad. The *Nancy* was carrying munitions. Two thousand muskets, plenty of round shot, flints, musket balls—even a grand thirteen-inch brass mortar. When they hauled the monster ashore, ol' General Putnam christened it with a flagon of rum."

Paul smiled. "A thirteen-inch mortar! Lord, wait until the British get a taste of *that!*"

"We'll have a long wait," Toby grumbled. "There's nary enough powder to fire it."

The boy frowned. For weeks now he'd heard rumors that the army was very short of gunpowder; one more battle and the supply would be gone. It was worrisome, if the rumors were true.

"Word's come," Toby added, "that powder's on the way from France and Spain. And a new powder mill's being built here in Canton. Your pa's been put in charge, 'n he's got old Jim Otis, the powder master, to help him. But it will be months afore they're turning out enough to supply everyone."

Silently they watched a British patrol frigate as it beat its slow way across the harbor. Then Paul asked, "Any news of my friend, Will Knox?"

Toby spat into the water. He looked around carefully before answering; then he grinned. "He and the colonel have took themselves off to Fort Ticonderoga. They're aiming to collect the cannons up there and bring 'em back to headquarters."

Paul was surprised. The Ticonderoga cannons! So *that* was the colonel's secret plan—and a mighty clever one!

"Those big guns," he said, "will be useful when they get here."

Toby shot him a grim look. "*If* they get here, lad. *If.*"

Paul bridled. "I'm not worried. The colonel will have many a good hand with him."

The boatman nodded. "Aye, but the one he needs is the hand of Providence."

Later, walking home through the dreary streets, Paul heard the church bells again. The mournful ringing troubled him. Old Toby wasn't very hopeful about Colonel Knox's journey. It *did* seem a bit daft, Paul admitted—well nigh unworkable. He turned and looked toward Charlestown and the Mystick River. Somewhere, miles beyond Boston, his friend Will was helping to haul cannons over the mountains to save the rebel cause. It was a dangerous mission and a daring one. But would it succeed, or would it end in failure?

*None can say*, chimed the bells. *None can say . . . none can say . . .*

# 10
# Heading Overland

The first run from Fort George to Glens Falls was only ten miles, but to Will Knox it seemed like ten times ten.

This was rough terrain—the foothills of the Adirondack Mountains, far from civilization. There were no highways here. No paved roads. No bridges or underpasses. No route signs or sheltered rest areas or lighting to chase the gloom. What passed for a road was only a dirt trail, used now and then by farmers, trappers, or migrating Indians. In summer the trail was often a sea of mud. Now, in the icy cold, it was a frozen crisscross of ruts and ridges, as hard as the granite rocks of the mountain.

With so many vehicles plus the animals needed to pull and drag them, the colonel's "noble train of artillery" was spread out for almost a mile. William was in charge of a heavy gun bringing up the rear of the convoy. His brother, riding a sorrel mare, trotted up and down the line, watching for trouble spots and helping stragglers.

The guns crawled slowly along the bumpy route, and every yard was hard work. Wagon wheels creaked. Drivers cracked their whips. Oxen strained. Horses whinnied. Men swore and shouted, sweating under their wool shirts while their breath came out in icy clouds.

The Beckers' wagon, with its brass cannon, was near the middle of the convoy. Sitting beside his father, J. P. watched the careful way the old veteran handled the team. Controlling four horses on this kind of rough trail took nerve and skill. Half rising from his seat, reins threaded through his strong fingers, Becker guided the animals, calming and coaxing them.

Suddenly, as they topped a hill, their lead horse stumbled on a sharp rock. "Look out!" Becker shouted. The heavy wagon lurched to one side; J. P. slid from his perch and landed hard on the ground. He got up dizzily, rubbing a sore hip—but his pride was wounded more than his body. Colonel Knox rode up and was relieved to see that J. P. wasn't seriously hurt. But the wagon had skidded off into a ditch.

Half a dozen troopers were needed—with Becker handling the horses—to get the heavy cart back on the trail. By the time the cart was righted and ready to move, the front half of the convoy had lumbered ahead, leaving a wide gap in the line.

The accident led to a change in the rules. "From now on," Henry announced at the next rest stop, "when a unit gets in trouble, the whole caravan will halt. That way we'll keep everyone close together. And we'll have enough manpower in case there's serious trouble."

Day faded into dark as the convoy struggled on, and by the time they reached Glens Falls, men and animals were bone weary. The strange parade received a wonderful welcome from the villagers—certainly the artillery train was the most exciting thing that had ever happened to this tiny, out-of-the-way place. The animals were quickly unhitched, fed, watered, and given shelter. The men were treated to great platters of hot food, and warm dry beds were found for them in barns and farmhouses.

The town had a small inn, a coach stop for travelers, and the innkeeper bustled about tidying a room for Colonel Knox. After a good meal washed down with hot cider, Henry met with Will and the other convoy leaders. Their next goal was to cross the upper Hudson and turn south to Saratoga.

"The river's frozen solid, so we won't have any trouble crossing," the colonel said.

Will chimed in, "The locals say snow's on the way. I expect a good fall of wet snow'd make it easier for the sleds."

His brother nodded. "You're right. We can move twice as fast over snow, if it's not *too* heavy. So let's gamble. We'll wait here a bit—and pray for a white Christmas."

# 11

# Into the Storm

On Christmas Eve, Henry Knox got his wish: it finally began to snow. Fat white flakes fell steadily, blanketing the trails and adorning the branches of the pines. Early Christmas morning the men rolled out of their warm beds, washed up, ate a quick breakfast, and harnessed the animals. Eager to begin, Henry gave the signal and the guns crept slowly out of Glens Falls.

Just below town, where the Hudson made a loop, the river was solidly frozen. With relief, Will saw that the ice was very thick—thick enough to carry the heavy sleds and carts. The good crust of snow would give traction for the animals. The drivers all made this crossing safely, then they headed for Saratoga. From there the colonel hoped to push right on to Albany.

The recent snow had been a big help and the men were in good spirits. At the rear of the column, Henry rode alongside William's sled with its giant twenty-four-pounder.

"If our luck holds," he said, "we'll be right on schedule, little brother. No doubt about it—the general will have his cannons in two more weeks."

Will, watching the colonel trot to the front of the line, shook his head and smiled. That's what he liked about Henry—the man was always so cheerful and optimistic, so sure everything would work out. As far as Colonel Knox was concerned, bad luck was something that only happened to *other* folks.

Henry passed the Beckers' wagon and gave them a friendly wave. Perched high on his seat, J. P. could see the whole column. Craning his neck, he could even spy Will Knox, whom he admired, bringing up the rear. The drivers in their gray scarves and caps, the troopers in their blue tunics, the guns of iron and glowing brass, the sleek muscles of the straining horses, the shiny leather harnesses, the brown oxen bending under wooden yokes—everything stood out crystal-sharp against the dazzling snow. John P. Becker decided that he'd never seen a grander sight.

When they reached Saratoga the tired men received a welcome much like the one at Glens Falls. It looked to William as if everyone in town came running to greet them. And in the spirit of Christmas, people brought baskets of food and jugs of ale and cider.

The next morning the men started out again. But as they moved through the Hudson Valley, leaving the Adirondacks behind, their luck changed. Instead of stopping, the snow began to fall more heavily—and slowly their kind helper became an ugly enemy.

The temperature dropped, the wind rose, and eight miles below Saratoga the convoy found itself smack in the middle of a raging storm. Waves of snow fell and a howling wind whipped stinging needles of ice into the faces of men and animals. It piled up giant drifts that blocked the trail. Time after time, Will and the others had to climb down and shovel the drifts away before they could push on.

Along with this came bitter, bone-chilling cold. Huddled on the seat, leaning against his father, J. P. thought he would never feel warm again. He'd wrapped pieces of burlap over his shoes, but his feet were blocks of ice. His hands were numb in their wool gloves, even tucked inside his coat pockets. And his wide-brim hat was yanked so far down over his frozen ears that he couldn't see anything in front of him. Not that there was anything to see through the fierce driving sleet.

Henry and Will did their best to keep the convoy moving. Horses and oxen struggled bravely through ten inches of snow. Then twelve inches. Then eighteen inches. Soon the animals were fighting through snow well over two feet deep. At that point, though the solid oxen still tried to move, the horses could not go on; strain as they would, the snow was simply too thick.

In the teeth of this blizzard, the convoy came to a dead halt and Henry called a conference. "We're just north of the town of Stillwater," he said. "Some of us will have to get through to the town on foot and bring help."

The animals were unhitched and led into a grove of pine trees where they had a little shelter. Most of the men, with Will in charge, stayed to build fires, guard the wagons, and tend the weary animals. The rest of the party, led by Henry, started hiking.

From the grove, William watched the hikers disappear in a blinding whirl of white. For the first time during the trip, the young soldier felt a pang of doubt, a nagging feeling that they might fail. He fought the unpleasant feeling, but it kept returning to torment him. Standing there with sleet stinging his face, he began to wonder if their "noble train of artillery" had finally come to the real end of the line.

# 12

# A New Start

The rescue party trudged blindly through the storm, and even for a husky six-footer like Henry Knox, it was a grueling march. For several miles they struggled through snow three feet deep, against a howling wind, moving across country with no path or trail to guide them. Their breath came in gasps and they floundered in deep drifts, often losing their footing.

At last, exhausted and numb with cold, they staggered into Stillwater and were taken to the home of Squire Fisher. Bowls of hot broth eaten in front of an open fire helped to revive the frozen hikers. When the squire heard Henry's story, he sent his farmhands with food and supplies to relieve the crew trapped in the pine grove. Then he lent Henry his fastest horse so the colonel could race ahead to Albany.

Meanwhile, in the snowbound grove, Will did his best to keep the animals warm and raise the men's failing spirits.

He joked with young J. P., who was feeling frightened but trying hard not to show it.

By evening the storm had passed and the wind finally died down. Henry, riding the fast mount, managed to reach Albany at last and hurried to see General Schuyler. The general, who was one of the doubters, still thought the plan was crazy. But he admired the colonel's stubborn courage.

"Most of the horses are played out and have to be replaced," Henry said unhappily. "Some of our men are sick, too, and need medical help."

Schuyler nodded thoughtfully. "We'll take care of your sick. I'll also send a platoon into the countryside to find substitutes. I don't know how much luck we'll have, but we'll try."

Henry Knox had been authorized to pay twelve shillings a day for each span of horses he hired. It was a good fee, but he found to his dismay that there were few takers. The locals all supported the rebel cause, but they knew the perils of winter and the dangers of the trail, and they were afraid to risk their animals.

While Henry fretted over the delay, Schuyler's men scoured the area, visiting every farm and hamlet, bargaining for teams and drivers. It took four full days before enough replacements could be found and sent to Stillwater, where Will and the others were waiting. Here the changes were made and new teams were harnessed in place. Finally, on December 31, the convoy was ready to move ahead.

Their next goal was to get across the Mohawk River, which joined the Hudson near a town called Lansing's Ferry. The Mohawk was frozen over, and Henry expected this to be a simple operation like their earlier crossing. When they reached the riverbank, Will and several other men walked out on the ice. They drilled small holes here and there to test for thickness. Then they came back with long faces.

"The ice is starting to melt," Will explained to his brother. "It's getting thin out toward the middle."

Henry scratched his chin slowly. "You think it can hold the heavy wagons?" he asked.

Will shook his head unhappily. "Not a chance," he said. "I'm afraid they'll never make it."

# 13

# Good News for the British

While Henry Knox's cannon convoy was stalled at the Mohawk River, Major General William Howe, back in Boston, was busy making plans.

In his cabin aboard HMS *Somerset*, Sir William read a secret dispatch from London. He read it through, then read it again. Locking it in a desk drawer, he leaned back and smiled. After so many disappointments, it was nice to have good news.

Muffled against the cold, the British commander stepped on deck and looked around the harbor. Like faithful watchdogs his ships were all in place, standing guard over the helpless city. Howe began to pace alongside the ornate railing, reviewing in his mind the events that had recently taken place.

Two weeks ago, in mid-December, transports had sailed in from England bringing a regiment of marines. Then other ships had arrived from the Bay of Fundy in Canada, carrying hay and grain for the horses. But the *real* supply convoy, the one he'd been counting on, had met with disaster. Twenty-six ships had left Plymouth, England, bound for Boston Harbor. They carried thousands of redcoats as well as cannons, powder, food, and muskets—everything the general was waiting for. Then in midocean the convoy sailed into a hurricane. The ships were scattered and blown off course, and they wound up far to the south in the British West Indies.

During the storm many soldiers were lost and ships were damaged. Some had escaped without too much harm; but it would take a long time for these ships to be refitted, then to beat their way north in the middle of winter.

Adding to Howe's problems, he had to deal with the cursed little ships called privateers. These weren't part of an official navy, but the rebel congress allowed them to capture any British vessels that came their way. To the colonists the raiders were heroes, but to General Howe the armed privateers were plain pirates—lawless ships that stole out of port and attacked his merchantmen, then took cover in the many bays and inlets of New England. The privateers not only captured Howe's cargoes, but then escaped to shallow waters where his warships couldn't follow.

All in all, 1775 had been a black year for Sir William—a year filled with trouble. But the secret dispatch that had just arrived gave him hope. According to this message a new supply fleet was being assembled, even larger than the last. After the start of the new year, this convoy would cross the Atlantic with the reinforcements he needed. In a neat, flowery hand the secretary of the admiralty had promised Howe 40,000 troops plus enough weapons to carry out all his plans ". . . for 1776, and up to May of 1777."

The general returned to his cabin to study his maps. He could rely on the Admiralty. If the weather behaved, the transports and supply ships would arrive soon. Then, with a powerful new force, he would strike. He was tired of the stalemate. Tired of the inactivity. Tired of the fool rebels with their prattle about "freedom" and "liberty."

Sir William Howe could hardly wait to crush Washington and the colonial army once and for all.

# 14

# Dangerous Ice

Henry and his men spent the first day of 1776 trying to strengthen the ice on the Mohawk. To begin with, they laid out the shortest route across the river. Then at certain spots the men chopped holes through the ice. Water gushed up from these holes and flowed across the surface. In the cold wintry air the water froze quickly, adding a new layer of ice to what was there before.

The crew did this several times until the ice had built up and thickened. Now it was stronger—but would it be strong enough? Will stepped out onto the river. He walked up and down, frowning. "It *might* hold the big loads," he said to his brother, "but I'm not powerful sure."

Henry shrugged. "We won't know until we try. But we'll move the guns one at a time, starting with the lightest. Tell the drivers that *no* team is to go until the one before is safe on the other side."

The colonel had a long rope tied to the front of each sled

and wagon. The other end was attached to the harness of the team that did the hauling. A man walked alongside this rope, holding a sharp axe.

Colonel Knox climbed on the first sled and took the reins. "Keep an eye on that rope," he said to the man with the axe. "If the sled breaks through the ice, cut the rope fast. Then if it goes down, the load won't drag the team along with it. But you'll have to look sharp."

Everyone stood on the bank, watching tensely as Henry snapped his reins. The horses leaned into the traces and stepped out on the ice. It crackled a few warnings, but it managed to hold. Carefully, foot by slow foot. the sled moved across the frozen river. Sweating in spite of the cold, Henry talked to the horses, coaxing them. William bit his lip anxiously. J. P. Becker held his breath. The sled passed the halfway mark and drew near the far shore. In a few more minutes—though it seemed like hours to the men— the gun was across and the horses scrambled to safety.

Henry hopped down and joyously waved his hat. Will and the others cheered wildly and hurried to get the next sled ready. Then, one by one, horses and oxen—tethered to the long taut rope—hauled the cargo across. And every step of the way, the man with the axe stood ready in case of danger.

The river passage took all afternoon. Finally every load was across the Mohawk except for three cannons—the heaviest of all. These were Henry's pride and joy, the most important of his weapons, and he wanted to be sure they would make it across safely. So he had fresh holes chopped along the route. In the gathering darkness, river water gushed from the holes and swept across the ice.

"By morning the new layer should be frozen fine," Henry said to Will. "Then we'll try crossing the big guns."

———

That night, after supper and hot coffee brewed over the campfire, the men sat around smoking their pipes and staring into the flames. One of the soldiers took a wooden fife from his tunic and began to play softly. J. P., sitting with a warm blanket around his shoulders, recognized the tune. The "Liberty Song" was a great favorite among the colonists; in fact some thought of it as their new anthem. A few troopers began to sing, and the boy listened happily to the stirring words:

> *Come join hand in hand, brave Americans all,*
> *And rouse your bold hearts at fair Liberty's call;*
> *No tyrannous acts shall suppress your just claim,*
> *Or stain with dishonor America's name . . .*

As the sound of the fife slid into the chorus, others added their voices:

> *In Freedom we're born*
> *And in Freedom we'll live.*
> *Our hearts are ready,*
> *Steady, friends, steady—*
> *Not as slaves but as Freemen*
> *Our strength we will give!*

The campfire blazed in the night air. Orange flames leaped high into the black sky, their brightness echoing the bright hopes of a country struggling to be born.

At daybreak the men prepared for the test. The first of the huge guns, hauled by four pair of oxen, was eased carefully onto the frozen river. The ice creaked and cracked as if complaining about its burden. But the extra thickness worked. The surface held.

When this gun was across, the second cannon was moved without incident. Finally there was only the twenty-four-pounder left. This was Will's gun, and he wouldn't allow anyone else to take it across. He climbed aboard the sled and guided the oxen out onto the ice. The creaking sounds grew louder and more menacing. Will sat tensely, hardly daring to breathe. The axe man, walking alongside, looked nervous and tested the sharpness of his blade.

The oxen passed the halfway point. Slowly, they inched closer and closer to the far shore. Henry started to breathe a sigh of relief.

*Crack! Crack!*

The noise came sharp and loud, almost like gunfire. A great black gap opened in the ice. Will jumped from the sled. The axe man leaped forward, swung his blade, and parted the rope. As the gun went under, the oxen, suddenly free of their load, reacted with fear. They lunged forward, trying to reach safety. J. P.'s father, who was standing nearby, dove at the harness to keep the clumsy animals under control. He was yanked forward, where he tripped over a tree root and fell to the ground.

The old farmer lay on the frozen shore, holding his shoulder and gasping. J. P. rushed over, his face pale with alarm.

A soldier who had been trained as a medical orderly also hurried over. He knelt down and examined the groaning man.

"It's naught serious," he said. "He's throwed his shoulder out. I can put it to rights, but he'll need a sling. Afraid he won't be able to use the arm for a few days."

While the trooper went to work on Mr. Becker, Henry and Will took a look at the sunken cannon. Luckily it had gone down near the bank where the river was shallow, and parts of the gun and cart were showing above the surface. Colonel Knox was not about to abandon his finest prize.

"Bring plenty of rope and get some teams ready," he said to Will. "We're going to haul her out."

For the rest of the afternoon the men strained and sweated, hauling on ropes, prying at the gun with stout poles, urging the animals on. Little by little the monster crept free of the Mohawk's icy clutches and came to rest at last on the muddy bank.

Worn out from the day's work, the crew camped right there at the river's edge. Hollow-eyed, they ate supper quickly and were soon asleep. All except J. P. His father now felt better, but the boy sat beside him, keeping a drowsy watch.

At dawn the farmer, his arm in a sling, met with Colonel Knox. With the arm strapped, there was no way he could control the horses hitched to the Beckers' wagon. Henry scratched his chin. His drivers were all needed elsewhere; he had nobody else to spare. J. P., standing nearby, cleared his throat and tugged at his father's shirt. Becker grinned. "I know what's on your mind, John. You think you can handle four horses?"

J. P. nodded quickly. "Sure I can, Pa, if you'll ride next to me. I'll do everything just the way *you* did."

Colonel Knox was anxious to solve the problem, so he smiled his approval. "Fine, son. Fine. Then it's settled." With a nod he hurried off to organize the rest of the caravan.

Minutes later, Henry trotted by on his mare and signalled for the convoy to begin. With his father beside him, J. P. snapped his reins and called to the horses—trying to do it just as the older man had done—and the animals moved ahead obediently. As the long line of vehicles lumbered away from the frozen river, John thought he would burst with pride. He wasn't an onlooker anymore; he was a real team member now, doing his bit for the great cause.

# 15

# Marking Time

General Washington stepped back from the flagpole and saluted. Behind him, the regiments were drawn up. A squad fired a volley in the air and the men presented arms. Then the fife and drum corps marched smartly across the parade ground. At the edge of the field they turned and broke into a rousing version of the "Liberty Song."

The red, white, and blue ensign, just raised by the commander, was the very first flag of the colonial cause. It was called the "Grand Union" flag, and it snapped bravely in the Cambridge breeze, telling the world that the American colonies were now a nation and no longer subjects of Britain's king.

The day this ceremony took place was the very day that Henry and his men, far to the north, were dragging their sunken cannon out of the Mohawk River. Back at his desk after the flag-raising, Washington thought about Henry's artillery train. He reread a report just in from the hardworking colonel. The guns were on their way, but they were moving very slowly. Because of bad weather and worse terrain, Henry wrote, it would take longer to deliver them than he'd thought.

Washington ran a tired hand over his eyes. It had been a bad winter for the Continental Army, just as it had been for Howe and the redcoats. For one thing, Washington had to deal with thousands of New England troops who were quitting camp. They had enlisted at the beginning of July for six months—now their tour of duty was over. The worried officers tried hard to get their men to reenlist, but only a fraction did, for there was no reenlistment bounty. "The military chest is totally exhausted," Washington wrote to Philadelphia. "The paymaster has not a single dollar in hand."

But the lack of bonus money wasn't as bad as the lack of morale. The colonial troops were tough and independent. They had joined the army with high hopes; now they were cold, homesick, disillusioned, and angry at the long stalemate. For some, patriotism had become an empty word. Nothing was happening. British or no British, they were going home to their shops, farms, and families.

Trying to keep his army from melting away, Washington suggested attacking the redcoats in Boston. But he was overruled by congress and the War Council: without enough powder and artillery, a head-on attack was too risky. So the general had to settle for strengthening his lines and capturing an outpost called Cobble Hill.

The weeks dragged on, but by the beginning of 1776 the worst seemed over. New men and officers came pouring in to replace the ones who'd left for home, and the army grew to over 10,500 men. This was very satisfying, but numbers meant little without the power of weapons. Washington, like his British enemy, was still playing a waiting game. General Howe waited for a military convoy crossing the stormy Atlantic. General Washington waited for an artillery convoy crawling from Fort Ticonderoga.

The question that worried George Washington on that January day was: which of the two convoys would arrive first?

# 16

# The Ghosts of Bloody Pond

They had been on the trail all day but Henry, trying to make up lost time, decided to push on a while longer. At that point the Beckers' wagon was up in front and J. P. was feeling pleased with himself. With only a little help from his pa, he'd managed the horses like an expert.

The heavy vehicles creaked slowly along the narrow trail on the west bank of the Hudson. It was growing dark, and a white mist was creeping across the river. J. P.'s father dozed on the seat beside him. Over his shoulder the boy could see the other sleds and carts following behind. The drivers and soldiers were surprisingly quiet. Even the animals seemed to doze in their traces as they trudged along.

A pale half-moon rose, winking through the pines, while the mist crept in and out of the dark branches.

*Caw! Caw! Caw!* A flight of crows exploded from the trees, complaining loudly at the human intruders. Somewhere an owl hooted, getting ready to hunt for his supper.

J. P. was feeling tired. He was also vaguely uneasy. Looking around, he noticed some landmarks and recognized where he was. Twenty years ago this part of the countryside had been a bloody battleground. It was during the French and Indian wars—a time when French troops and their Indian allies fought the British for control of New England and Canada. The British had finally won, but only after years of heavy fighting.

On this very spot there had been a fierce battle—J. P. had heard the whole story from the old-timers. The fight had raged all day long, seesawing back and forth, and there were many killed on both sides. Some of the bodies had been flung into a nearby pond. It was known ever since as Bloody Pond—and folks said the forest was haunted by the ghosts of those who wouldn't stay down in their watery grave.

Inching along with the pines looming overhead, J. P. remembered the grisly tale. His eyes were heavy with sleep, and in the gloom he thought he could almost see the flitting shades of Bloody Pond. He stifled a cry. Yes, there they were! French soldiers in blue and British in red, their uniforms torn and bloodied . . . fierce Iroquois wielding war axes . . . painted Mohawks with dripping scalps dangling from their belts! The phantoms were all around him, fighting one another, gliding in and out of the dank mists . . .

J. P. held his breath and listened. Now he heard, ever so faintly, the sound of Indian war whoops, the snap of muskets, and the screams of the dying. Or were they just the usual noises of the night forest?

The boy shivered. He shook his head to clear away the frightening, ghostly images.

Suddenly his two lead horses reared and whinnied in fear. There was a scuffle of hooves as the second pair reacted to them nervously. J. P. tugged hard at the reins. His father woke with a start and dove forward to help. Behind them, the next driver pulled in his team with an oath, barely avoiding a pileup. Meanwhile the spooked horses kept bucking and snorting, refusing to move ahead.

"Hold steady, John!" his father cried. "Hold steady!"

"It's the ha'nts, pa!" J. P. gasped. "Bloody Pond! The horses can see 'em!"

Questions were being shouted up and down the line. Some troopers raced over with a lighted torch, and Colonel Knox rode up anxiously.

The troopers ran to the front of the Beckers' wagon and bent down. In a moment they stood up, holding a young colonial soldier between them. The man's hair was matted, his uniform was muddy, and he wore a foolish grin. He also reeked of brandy. When dragged to the side of the trail and doused with water, he came slowly out of his drunken stupor. Questioning him, the colonel learned that the man was from nearby Fort Lyman. Making his way back to camp he'd lost his way, and decided to have a quiet nap in the middle of the trail.

"Blasted fool!" Will Knox shouted. He grabbed the soldier's coat, gave him a tongue-lashing, and started him back to the fort with a well-placed kick.

Grinning, the colonel took off his hat and wiped his brow. "I guess we've had enough ruckus for one day," he said. "Pass the word—we'll make camp here."

After supper, J. P. rolled himself gratefully in his blankets. Luckily, nobody but his father had heard his frightened panicky outburst. No harm was done and he was glad that his ghosts had turned out to be merely a drunken soldier. Still, John Becker would be very happy in the morning to turn his back on Bloody Pond.

# 17

# South to Claverack

Will and his brother stood on the bank and stared at the river, which was choked with ice floes. William began to sing an old folk song:

> *The water is wide, I cannot cross,*
> *And neither have I wings to fly.*
> *Build me a boat that can carry two,*
> *And we shall row, my love and I!*

The colonel grunted and waved his hand. "We'll need more than a boat to get across *this* mess. We'll need a whole fleet. Sometimes I think the weather gods have turned Royalist on us!"

South of Albany the convoy was at a halt again. According to plan they were supposed to go back across the Hudson at this point. On the other side they would pick up the Old

Post Road, a smooth route that could take them quickly to the town of Kinderhook. But their bad luck was continuing: a sudden thaw had set in and the river ice had started to break up. It was now a mass of huge floes moving sluggishly downstream. There was no solid place where the teamsters could cross, and there were no barges nearby—not that they could have been much use on the ice-clogged river.

Henry shook his head, staring at the ice floes that seemed to taunt him. For the first time since Lake George, he felt doubts about the plan. But he forced himself to sound confident. "If we don't cross here," he said, "we'll have to go miles out of the way. And we've lost too much time already. We'll stay put and pray for another freeze."

Muttering to himself, he stomped over to the farmhouse serving as his headquarters. At the kitchen table he sat down and wrote another letter to Lucy, whom he deeply missed. Then he sent a report to General Washington, which would go to Cambridge by courier. In it he wrote:

The want of snow detained us for some days, and now a cruel thaw hinders us from crossing the Hudson River . . . The first severe night will make the ice sufficiently strong. Till that happens, the cannon and mortars must remain where they are . . . which pains me exceedingly.

After forty-eight hours of impatient waiting—which kept J. P. and everyone else on edge—the freeze finally came. The next morning, the river was solid and the vehicles made their way slowly across the ice, going around the craggy floes that jutted up here and there.

Once on the Old Post Road the men moved along at a steady pace. They reached Kinderhook without mishap, though some of the horses were trail-weary and had to be replaced. After resting here for a while, the train forded a shallow branch of the Moosic River and headed south to Claverack.

For a while the travelers had better luck. They reached town by nightfall, and again the whole community turned out to greet them. Colonel Knox was cheered. Pleased with their progress—it had been their best day yet—he was looking forward to an early morning start.

Suddenly there was a loud cracking noise. A sled hauling the eighteen-pounder had been weakened by the journey; it collapsed in a shower of splinters and broken wood.

Henry and Will inspected the wreckage unhappily. Nobody had been hurt, but the vehicle looked like it had been smashed by a giant hammer. "We haven't any spare sleds," Henry sighed, "and that gun's too big to put on another load. We'll have to build a new sled—extra strong."

The colonel's plan wasn't as simple as he thought. First the right hardwood trees had to be located. Then they had to be cut down and sawed into planks and runners. Next, they had to find a local blacksmith to forge iron rims for the runners and bolt them in place. And finally, metal rings had to be attached to hold the harnesses. Henry growled over the delay. It took two full days to build and load the new vehicle; then at last he gave the signal, and they started on their way.

Leaving Claverack and the Hudson Valley behind, the caravan crossed into Massachusetts. Ahead lay the roughest part of the trip, the Berkshire Mountain range. Here the tired men would face one hundred miles of wild country— steep hills and deep ravines, treacherous gorges and streams filled with jagged rocks. For most of the way there were absolutely no roads or trails, not even crude footpaths.

As they pushed on to Great Barrington, Will Knox studied

the looming hills. He felt nervous and worried. The caravan was way behind schedule and now they faced their biggest challenge. Some instinct told the young soldier that these high rocky mountains—and not the British—were going to be their worst enemy.

# 18

# A Walk in the Rain

It was drizzling in Boston—a thin rain, more like cold mist. The two companions walked down Beacon Street, their jacket collars turned up, their shoulders hunched against the wetness.

Nearby, on the Common, a company of soggy redcoats was going halfheartedly through a drill. The walkers stopped to watch.

"They're a sorry-looking lot," Paul Junior whispered.

Old Toby grunted. "Part of Howe's reinforcements. Three troopships came in yesterday from England with a whole passel of new so'jers."

Paul frowned. "I was afeared of it. I saw the ships anchored off Hudson's Point this morning."

The old boatman spat in the muddy road. "There be rumors," he said in a low voice, "that England's having trouble getting volunteers. Not many British lads are keen on sailing the ocean to fight us on our home ground. I hear tell Bow-wow Howe's had to scrape the bottom of the barrel."

Paul studied the marines, drilling carelessly. "Looks to me like they're half-starved."

Toby nodded. "Aye, it's the thin rations. But I'll tell you something, lad—their *cannons* aren't going hungry; there's plenty o' powder to feed *them*. And now it looks like the British have 'most as many fighting men as Gen'l Washington."

The strollers, one young and vigorous, the other old and hobbling, went past John Hancock's mansion on the slope of Beacon Hill. Hancock, a rebel leader wanted by the British, was safe in Philadelphia. But one of Howe's aides, General Henry Clinton, was using the Hancock home as a headquarters, so it had been spared destruction.

The drizzle finally ended and the walkers turned into Cornhill Street, where Henry Knox once had his bookshop. Near the Old State House they leaned against a mossy wall and the boatman lit his pipe. He looked up and down carefully, then leaned over to his young friend. "Look you, Master Paul. Washington's had another dispatch from Colonel Knox. Your friend Will and his cannons have got as far as Claverack. I'd say that's nigh on halfway. Now they must come east over the mountains."

Paul was excited at the news. "I keep hoping and praying they'll reach Cambridge soon," he sighed. "Do *you* think they'll make it?"

The old-timer squinted up at the clouded sky. "Can't rightly say. But if they don't, Boston's done for."

The city was gloomy and half-deserted. A few people in drab clothing hurried by, their faces thin and pale. Paul tried to shift to a cheerier note. "Toby, I had a mind to ask you—what does the new flag look like?"

The boatman's old face crinkled into a smile. "The

71

'Grand Union' flag? She's mortal fine, lad. I was right there when Gen'l Washington raised 'er for the first time. She's got red and white stripes—thirteen of 'em, one for each colony. And in the upper corner—the canton, they calls it—there's a small Union Jack, for ol' time's sake." The veteran shook his head with wonder. "I tell you, son, it's powerful good to see our own flag flying in the breeze over Cambridge."

Paul looked around at the sad, gray city. "You think," he asked wistfully, "we'll ever see it flying here over Boston?"

Toby trudged along, chewing moodily on his pipe, and gave no answer.

# 19

# The Runaway

"Heave away-ho! Heave away-ho!"

The men bent their backs to the job while Will called the tempo. When the gun was halfway up the slope he signalled a pause. Holding the taut rope with one hand, he used the other to dash sweat from his eyes. He was dripping wet in spite of the cold. His back ached and his shoulders burned with pain.

After a short rest, Will grabbed the rope with both hands and started his crew working again.

"Heave away-ho! Heave away-ho!"

The teamsters had been at it all day, struggling through an area called Greenwoods—a twelve-mile stretch thick with evergreen trees. There were no marked routes here, only a vague Indian footpath snaking across hill and dale.

"There's no way around all of this," Henry had said to Will. "No possible detour. We have to imitate the Indians— go straight up and over."

First the men cut down the smaller trees and chopped away the underbrush, creating a wide path up the steep incline. Then, one by one, with extra men on each side to help, the lighter loads were pulled up the slope by the animals. It was slow going, but finally the small guns were all at the top.

A different plan was needed for the heavy cannons. The horses and oxen were unhitched and led up the slope. Then the big weapons were rigged with long ropes. These were carried up the hill, looped around stout trees, and brought back down to the work parties. Finally each gun was hauled up pulley-style, inch by inch.

Will and his crew had been hoisting a thirteen-pounder, and they were relieved when the gun finally reached the summit. Nearby a second party was at work, raising a giant brass siege mortar, and they chanted together as they heaved on the straining rope.

Resting on the ground, Will watched the mortar crew. Young John Becker was climbing toward them, carrying a bucket and a tin dipper.

"Pa thought you all might fancy a drink," J. P. said to William. Gratefully, the men gulped the clear spring water and some tipped the dipper over their heads, letting the cool liquid run over their sweaty faces and necks. After they'd had their fill, J. P. hefted his bucket and started toward the next group.

"*Ho! Look out!*"

There were sudden shouts and loud crashes. Everyone turned and stared. The rope holding the siege mortar had parted—the gun came hurtling down the hillside!

Shouting and swearing, the men scrambled as the heavy gun crashed downhill. It fell like a juggernaut, a mad brass beast, bounding and bouncing wildly off rocks and tree stumps.

*Smash! Crack! Boom!*

Down it came, faster than fear, a solid ton of doom crushing everything in its way. J. P., carrying his water bucket, saw the mortar racing toward him. As he turned to run, his foot caught on a tree root and he went sprawling.

Will streaked toward J. P. He dove, grabbed him, and fell to one side with the boy as the juggernaut hurtled by, missing them by inches. The bucket that J. P. had dropped was smashed to splinters.

With a thud the cannon came to rest in the stream at the foot of the hill. Its muzzle gaped at the sky. The young boy coughed and sat up slowly, the breath knocked out of him. There was a gash on his forehead, and blood trickled down his cheek. Grunting, Will also sat up, clutching a badly bruised knee.

The men came running. They crowded around, all talking at once as they helped the dazed pair to their feet. J. P. thanked Will haltingly, stumbling shyly over his words. Pa Becker grabbed Will's hand and pumped it vigorously. Henry pounded him on the back. "That was quick thinking," he said to Will. The colonel tried to sound gruff, but he beamed with pride at his young brother.

Later they climbed down the hill and looked at the runaway cannon lying in the stream.

"This is the last one," the colonel said, "so let's start moving it. And this time I want it double-roped."

With the mortar finally rigged, Will, still limping, insisted on pacing the crew. He grabbed the rope while the others fell in behind him. Then he began to chant:

"Heave away-ho! Heave away-ho!"

The brass mortar crept slowly up the rough slope. Will Knox's strong voice, calling the time, rose in the mountain air and drifted through the silent pines.

# 20

# The Chasm

From an upper window at headquarters, Washington could see Howe's troopships in the harbor. For a while he studied them with his telescope, then closed the glass and went downstairs.

Outside his office door the sentry snapped to attention. Washington took note of the man's smart appearance and drew comfort from it. Yes, the Continental Army was making progress; it was beginning to look like a real fighting force. But they still needed artillery in order to fight.

At his desk Washington stared at the calendar and frowned. Time was running out. From his spies in Boston, he knew that the British reinforcements weren't top-grade troops—but there were quite a lot of them. Enough now for Howe to launch his attack.

The commander drummed his fingers on the desk. Where in blazes was Knox with his cannons? How much longer could they wait? Taking a fresh sheet of paper, he began a note to General Schuyler in Albany. He mentioned the enemy's reinforcements, which worried him. Then he confided: "I am in hopes that Colonel Knox will arrive with the artillery in a few days. *It is much needed.*"

The general would have been even more worried if he knew that while he sat writing, Henry and his men were facing another crisis.

The convoy had fought its way over the hills, past the mountain hamlet of Otis and the village of Blanford. Their next goal was Westfield, on the east slope of the Berkshire range. From Westfield the path would be easier, but right now they were on the rim of a steep chasm that dropped straight down for hundreds of feet.

The travelers were at a dead halt. They'd met up with bad terrain before, but never anything this dangerous.

Standing at the edge looking over, the drivers shook their heads and grumbled to each other. Finally an old-timer named Thorne spoke up. " 'Tain't any way to get down *this* cliff, Colonel. No sir! Not a man among us says it can be done."

Henry frowned. "I know it's bad. But the ridge runs south clear into Connecticut. There's no way 'round—not for miles. We'll have to take a chance."

Thorne grunted. "All of us is strong for the cause, Colonel, but we didn't sign on for suicide."

Another driver chimed in. "Just gettin' the animals down is nigh impossible. And if a load ever broke loose, there'd be blue ruin for sure."

The argument went back and forth. For almost three hours Henry coaxed and pleaded, but the men wouldn't budge. Will began to think that the mission was doomed; all their work had been for nothing. But the colonel refused to quit, and finally his stubbornness—plus some practical new ideas from Will—saved the day: the men agreed at last to tackle the chasm, though few of them expected to succeed.

William's plan of action matched the one they'd used before. But this time he added many safeguards. The animals were unhitched, then they were led, sliding and slipping, down the steep incline. Meanwhile the vehicles were rigged with heavy ropes which were looped around big trees. Drag chains and guy ropes were added to help the crews steady the loads as they went downhill.

Now, under the colonel's sharp eye, each gun was lowered little by little. Every fifty feet, fat logs were wedged under wheels and runners to hold the loads in place. Then the men ran ahead and shifted the heavy ropes to trees farther down the slope. The tricky process was then repeated.

J. P. Becker, working alongside the older hands, kept an eye on his hero, Will. In spite of his bad knee, the colonel's brother was everywhere, limping along the ridge, giving orders, testing ropes, making sure that every gun moved safely. The troopers and drivers, remembering the runaway cannon, worked hard and took no foolish chances. There were a few snags and tense moments, but no accidents.

As the long hours passed the men's confidence grew, and even Thorne had to admit that the colonel had been right. They were beating the chasm.

By nightfall the whole artillery train was safely at the foot of the great hill. Not a single gun had been lost nor a man injured—and at that point, Henry called a halt.

"I'm right proud of us all," he said to the crew. "Let's eat supper and get a night's rest."

It was *one* decision over which there were no arguments.

# 21

# On to Westfield

At dawn the horses and oxen were hitched up, and the convoy started off. They followed a dry stream bed to a dirt trail. Henry knew from his map that the trail would take them straight to Westfield.

For a long while they had moved over hard frosty ground coated with snow—a smooth surface for the sled runners. But now the sun began beating down, melting the snow and turning the trail to mud. This made it slow going for the patient animals, who plodded along dragging their heavy loads. As usual, Colonel Knox fretted about losing time, but even *he* realized that the weather was something he couldn't give orders to.

Mr. Becker's shoulder was now healed, and he took over the reins of their wagon. J. P. was a little disappointed at losing his job, but Will saw this and invited the boy to ride with him on the big sled. Will's vehicle, hauled by eight oxen, carried a twenty-four-pounder that the men had nicknamed the "Old Sow." Young John was thrilled to be riding alongside his friend, and he watched with pleasure the skillful way Will handled his four pair of oxen.

To help pass the time, William taught J. P. a lively song called "The Derby Ram," which people said was a favorite of General Washington's. J. P. soon learned the words, and as they rode along he and Will sang together:

> As I went down to Derby
> On a market day,
> I met the biggest ram, sir,
> That ever was fed on hay.
>
> The wool on that ram's back, sir,
> Reached up to the sky.
> Eagles built their nest there,
> I heard the young ones cry.
>
> He had four feet to walk on, sir.
> He had four feet to stand.
> And every one of those feet, sir,
> Covered an acre of land.
>
> And it's true my lads,
> It's true my lads,
> I never was given to lie.
> If you'd a' been in Derby,
> You'd see the same as I!

By the time the caravan plodded into Westfield, everyone was in a festive mood. Once again, the whole population came out to meet them. Few of the locals had ever seen cannons before, and they marveled at the giant weapons tied on the carts. They also gave the travelers ale, cider, and all the good food they could eat.

At the town inn, Henry and Will relaxed and joined the fun. The brothers smiled at each other happily, suddenly aware that the worst of their ordeal was over. The ale flowed freely, and numerous toasts were offered. "Here's to Colonel Knox!" somebody shouted. "Here's to good old General Washington!" others cried. "Here's to the artillery train!" "Here's to the rebel cause, 'n to blazes with the British!" A farmer brought out a fiddle and someone else brought out a dulcimer. They played tunes such as "The Massachusetts Hop" and "The Road to Boston," and Will Knox, his knee all better, joined in a lively square dance called a quadrille.

Will was bursting with pleasure and excitement. Henry was also pleased, but he tried to keep his emotions in check. "It looks right good," he admitted to Will, "but remember—we're not home *yet*."

As a climax to the festivities, Henry treated the townspeople to a demonstration. From their small supply he filled a powder horn and poured it into the breach of the Old Sow; then he put a match to the cannon's touchhole. The gun erupted in a powerful but harmless *BOOOM!* Everyone was impressed and cheered loudly.

"Thank the Lord," Will said to J. P. with a grin, "that the British are too far away to hear us!"

# 22

# Partings

The trip from Westfield to Springfield was a short one, but the trail was deep in mud so the pace of the convoy was slow.

As they drew near Springfield, the happy mood of the travelers changed to one of gloom. The reason was clear to William. Many of the drivers had agreed to stay with the train as far as Springfield. At that point—with the guns safely across the mountains—they were ready to return to their farms and towns in New York State. The men missed their families and were needed at home, but they had developed ties of loyalty to the mission and found it hard to tear themselves away.

Among those due to leave were the Beckers, who faced a long trip back to Glens Falls. They had been part of this venture day and night for over a month, and for J. P. it was painful to leave. When he said good-bye to William, he had to swallow hard to keep his voice steady. Will also felt sad, but he grinned, reached out, and ruffled J. P.'s hair. "Don't you mind, old friend," he said. "We'll meet up again, I promise. We'll have a proper visit after we send the redcoats packing."

At last Mr. Becker clucked to the horses and the empty wagon started off. J.P. turned around and watched the group standing near the vehicles. He kept watching longingly, until a bend in the trail hid the convoy from view.

Next morning, with new drivers and fresh oxen, the caravan pushed on through the thick mud. It was a long run to the next stop, the town of Worcester, but they made it at last and rested overnight.

Then at daybreak—like so many other daybreaks—Henry roused the men and led his convoy on to Framingham. They were now a mere twenty miles from Cambridge—and it suddenly dawned on Will that the journey was almost over. They really *had* done the impossible. The young man was elated, but Henry refused to relax. "We're not finished," he said. "I'll only rest easy when every gun is in place."

John Adams, a member of the Continental Congress (later to become the second president of the U.S.), was staying near Framingham. With his friend Elbridge Gerry, he hurried to town to inspect the new weapons. He was thrilled with what he saw, and that night wrote about it in his diary.

The next day, leaving Will in charge, Henry mounted a fast horse and raced to Cambridge to report. Washington and the others greeted him joyfully. And some of the officers apologized for having once doubted the "foolhardy" plan. They showered him with praise and compliments, all of which he shrugged off. "Sirs," he said with a smile, "if anyone deserves credit it's the drivers, the troopers, and those hardworking animals."

Later, at a council meeting, the mood grew serious. At

last they had good artillery and a big shipment of powder was on its way. But General Howe had also gained in strength. He commanded a huge army of redcoats, and his warships could still destroy Boston. The colonists would have to move very carefully. According to their spies, the British had no idea that the rebels had located heavy cannons. How could they guard this vital secret and keep the enemy in the dark? Now that they had real power, what was the best way to use it?

# 23
# Plans and Preparations

The first weeks of February 1776 were a time of feverish activity, all carried out in secret.

At Washington's orders, Colonel Knox brought some of the new guns, under cover of darkness, to Cobble Hill and Lechmere Point near the Cambridge lines. Others were set up around Roxbury. But the main gun batteries—and the big surprise for the British—would be elsewhere.

Near Roxbury, southwest of Boston Harbor, was a peninsula with steep hills known as Dorchester Heights. These ridges overlooked Boston and dominated the entire harbor. For some strange reason—though they had the troops and guns to do so—the British hadn't bothered to capture this strategic spot. Washington's plan was to put most of Henry's cannons here on the heights. But it had to be done secretly. If General Howe got wind of the rebels' activities, he would attack without delay.

Meanwhile the British commander stomped along the

deck of his warship, deep in his own plans. He now had 13,500 redcoats and tons of munitions—more than enough to launch a drive on Cambridge. But Howe was nervous about the weather. It was still winter; great windstorms often swept the harbor, and it would be dangerous to move his marines by boat. The rebels, he thought, were getting weaker and had no artillery—so it wouldn't hurt to wait a bit longer.

Unknown to smug General Howe, the colonists were working feverishly to get their guns all in place. Then one night toward the middle of the month, General Washington decided to probe the British defenses. Accompanied by Henry Knox and another colonel named Rufus Putnam, he left Roxbury on horseback. Later they dismounted and crept silently toward the causeway that crossed Boston Neck. The men moved carefully and quietly. Henry was enjoying the secret foray.

Suddenly two British officers came galloping toward them. The officers were waving their swords and signaling frantically to a British battery positioned near the town gates!

Washington and his men were startled. Colonel Knox grabbed his pistol, ready to defend the general. What fools they'd been, he thought. How careless! The British cavalrymen drew closer. The colonists turned, raced to their horses, leaped into the saddles, and galloped safely back to Roxbury. Henry shuddered when he thought of what might have happened if George Washington had been captured.

Narrow escape or not, General Washington was kept busy. A large shipment of powder had arrived, sent from France to New York, then brought overland. This, plus thousands of round shot taken from the captured brig, *Nancy*, meant plenty of ammunition for the Ticonderoga weapons.

Henry and Will worked day and night, and by the first of March they were able to report to the War Council that all was ready. General Washington's master plan could now begin.

On the night of March 2, cannons began firing steadily from the rebel lines north of Boston.

Paul Revere, Jr., reading by candlelight, heard them. Old Toby, rowing his skiff near the banks of the Charles River, heard them. Will Knox, working in Roxbury, heard them. And the British aboard their warships heard them, too.

General Howe, peering from the deck of HMS *Somerset*, was very surprised. Why were the fool colonials wasting powder when they had so little to spare? And where did they get those new guns? Well, no matter. If the rebels wanted an artillery duel, he'd jolly well oblige them. The British commander snapped orders to his adjutant, and soon the guns of the fleet began answering the rebel barrage.

For several hours cannons on both sides banged away loudly at each other, and the following night the duel was continued. Only light guns were being used, and in the darkness neither side did much damage. Which was just what Washington had expected. For the truth was, this sudden noisy barrage was simply a hoax—a clever diversion set up to fool the British and to draw their attention away from Dorchester Heights.

During the daylight hours Washington's ruse continued. He paraded an armed regiment along the ramparts of the Cambridge line as if preparing for battle. Knowing that spies would quickly tell the British, he assembled scores of wagons to carry the "wounded." He also turned the main Cambridge barracks into a hospital for use in the coming "attack."

The British easily took the bait. Unaware of Henry's

Ticonderoga prizes, Howe and his officers concentrated only on Cambridge. They paced the decks of their ships, studied the northern lines with their telescopes, and worried about the activities in that area.

While all this was going on, Henry and Will, with their artillerymen, worked like fiends to fortify Dorchester Heights. Washington had assigned many troopers, plus four hundred oxen, to the job of hauling the biggest guns up the steep hills and setting them in place. But winter winds had done their work. "The ground here is frozen solid," Henry said unhappily to Will. "It's like iron. We'll never be able to dig trenches."

Will frowned, his mind racing. "If we can't dig *down*, let's try building *up*."

The young soldier relished solving tough problems. In no time at all, he had his men gathering huge bundles of loose branches and tying them together tightly. These bundles were called "fascines." Placed upright, jammed one next to the other, the fascines formed a solid, musket-proof wall. He also had dozens of empty barrels rounded up and filled with rocks and sand. These were hauled up the hill and placed in front of the fascines. The heavy barrels gave strength to the makeshift wall. They also had another use: if Howe's marines stormed Dorchester Heights, the barrels, chained together, would be rolled downhill, smashing into the British lines.

Once this crude parapet was in place, openings were cut for the muzzles of the big guns. Then, one by one, the cannons were hauled uphill by straining teams of oxen. With so many men and animals to help, the work went swiftly. But Henry laid down strict rules of silence. Nobody was allowed to speak above a whisper. They used night lanterns, which shed only small patches of blue light, and straw was spread over the hillside to muffle the sound of the carts. Luckily, the wind was blowing from the west, carrying any sounds away from the British.

The men worked feverishly and quietly, under great pressure. The forts were going up right under the noses of Howe's redcoats, who were patrolling Boston Neck only a mile away. If they discovered the scheme, they would sound the alarm. British gunboats would race to the spot and destroy everything.

The work started right after dark and went on all through the long moonless night. Henry was on edge, but he tried to remain calm. This was his moment—the goal that he and Will had worked so hard for. With his brother at his side, the colonel was everywhere, up the hill and down, helping to load carts, pushing guns into position, and seeing that each post had a supply of shot and powder, and that each crew knew its duties. And all of this was done with signs, gestures, and quiet whispers.

Washington, anxious about the plan, moved his headquarters to Roxbury where he could keep in touch with the work on the ramparts. By four that morning, as the first glow of dawn appeared over the eastern bay, everything was finished. The heavy guns, including the runaway mortar and Will's giant twenty-four-pounder, were all in place.

Colonel Knox reported this to the commander, who nodded and smiled. But Washington's smile was an anxious one. So far things had gone smoothly. In the morning the rebels would face their final test.

# 24

# The Guns Speak

At daybreak on March 4, the watch officer aboard HMS *Somerset* was quietly pacing the quarterdeck. Glancing around the harbor, he happened to look toward Dorchester Heights. What he saw made his jaw drop and his eyes pop wide. He shouted for a messenger and sent him to awaken the British commander.

"Say that it's urgent!" the officer called as the messenger raced off.

General Howe hurried on deck, pulling a boat cloak over his nightshirt. By then the other officers were also on deck, all of them staring toward Dorchester. Howe followed their gaze and gasped in disbelief. There on the ridge—deserted and bare the day before—were two massive forts! As the first rays of wintry sun appeared, the watchers could see a long line of heavy cannons mounted on the parapet—and their muzzles were pointing straight at the British fleet!

Sir William Howe swore. He sputtered. He fretted and

fumed. What manner of black magic was this? How did the Yanks work such a miracle overnight? Where did those guns come from—and why hadn't the British sentries seen what was going on?

Looking for somebody to blame, Howe raved at his staff officers, who stood in a daze. Just then there was a long rolling of drums on the Dorchester ramparts.

Standing behind the fascines, General Washington nodded to Henry Knox. "Let's begin, Colonel," he said. Henry raised his arm and swung it down.

*Boooom! CRASH! Crack!*

With billowing smoke and flashes of flame, the guns of Ticonderoga spoke. They roared out, growling defiance at the enemy who, for so long, had tormented their city. Startled by the sounds, Paul and many other Bostonians pulled on clothes and raced to the waterfront to watch the spectacle and cheer wildly.

After the great opening salvo, Henry's guns were hauled in, sponged out, and reloaded with powder and shot. And once again they roared in loud triumph.

*Crash! BOOOOM!!*

The cannonade thundered across the harbor, sweeping over the city and rousing its citizens. In the rumbling, Will Knox heard a magic echo of things to come. To his ears, the blast was a song of victory . . . a mighty shout of freedom . . . a challenge to British rule . . . a roar of support for the colonies.

None of the cannons had been aimed and most of the shots fell harmlessly, sending up a forest of waterspouts around the blockading ships. But this was deliberate on Washington's part. His goal, at that point, wasn't to sink ships or take British lives. The Dorchester Heights gunfire was symbolic. Washington wanted a gesture of power— something to show the British the danger of their position.

His guns sent a strong message to the enemy: *The siege is over and the tide of battle has turned*.

General Howe was furious. He hated to accept defeat. Signal flags raced up the mainmast of the *Somerset*, giving orders to the fleet to return the rebel fire. Dutifully, the warships swung into position, bringing their broadside guns to bear on the audacious Yanks. Then a hundred British weapons belched fire and smoke, pouring shot after shot at Dorchester Heights.

Safe behind their barricade, Washington's men waited calmly. The British cannons were powerful, but they had limited movement. The colonists knew that the guns of the fleet couldn't be elevated high enough to damage the ramparts; in fact, Howe's barrage was useless. Try as they would, his gunners could barely reach halfway up the hillside, where their shots fell harmlessly.

For a while the British continued to waste powder and shot, but one by one the enemy guns began to fall silent. Washington studied the blockading ships and nodded to Henry Knox with satisfaction. In time—with careful attention to range and windage—the rebel cannons could sink the whole British fleet, ship by ship. But Howe still had cards to play. If he came under heavy attack, he might bombard the city and kill hundreds of innocent people. Even in defeat, his marines could torch Boston and burn it to the ground.

So the patriots had to move carefully. Washington's aim was to free the city and force the British out. He wanted victory, not tragedy—and now that he had artillery, victory was in his hands.

The sun crept higher while Henry's gunners stood by their weapons and waited. The last British cannon gave up and stopped firing. As the grim warships finally turned away from Dorchester, the men on the heights sent up a loud, ragged cheer. Somebody raised his voice in song, and soon a thousand joyous voices were added:

*Then join hand in hand, brave Americans all,*
*By uniting we stand, by dividing we fall.*
*In so righteous a cause let us hope to succeed.*
*For Heaven approves of each patriot's deed!*

Will Knox, his face streaked with powder and grime, came over and put an arm around his brother's shoulder. The two men looked at each other and grinned happily. They both had the same thoughts—and words weren't needed. The British were facing a clear defeat. Boston would now be free—and the brothers knew that some day the *rest* of America would also be free.

For the British rulers, this moment was the beginning of the end. For the American patriots, it was the end of the beginning.

# 25

# What Happened After

The minute General Howe saw the rebel cannons on Dorchester Heights, he knew the game was over. For a long while, with his redcoats and warships, he'd held the upper hand. But the colonists—those "country bumpkins" he'd once sneered at—had outplanned, outgunned, and outsmarted him.

Now the British had no choice: Henry's cannons had roared and the Royal Navy would have to quit Boston. But to save face, Howe tried a rearguard action. As the rebels expected, he made a halfhearted attempt to capture Dorchester with foot troops. A number of barges and longboats were assembled to carry the redcoats across the harbor. Then just as the boats were being loaded, a fierce storm came up.

The gale, lashing the harbor, was almost a hurricane—the kind of weather Howe feared. The barges were swamped, men were lost, and the commander called off the attack, which he suspected would have failed anyway.

The cat-and-mouse game was almost over, and messages began to pass between Howe's flagship and Washington's headquarters. There are no written notes or details of what was decided, but historians believe that a bargain was probably made: the British agreed not to destroy Boston, and in return the colonists allowed Howe's fleet to sail off unharmed.

It took a few days to round up extra British ships for this move. And at last, on March 17, the whole enemy armada scurried out of the harbor. With it went thousands of hated "lobsterbacks." Howe also took along about nine hundred Tory sympathizers who had stayed in Boston under British protection.

As Howe's sails vanished over the horizon, General Washington, with Colonel Knox at his side, led his victorious troops into the city. Boston was free at last, and people welcomed their liberators joyously. Drums rolled, fifes squealed, and there were happy celebrations everywhere from the Town Gates to Barton's Point, from Clark's Shipyard to Griffin Wharf.

The wonderful news spread quickly, and soon refugees came pouring in from all over the countryside. Lucy Knox hurried from Worcester by fast coach to join her now famous husband. Cartloads of food also came rumbling into town, to feed the hungry Bostonians who had been living on near-starvation diets.

Later in the day, at an inn near North Square, the two old friends, Will Knox and Paul Revere, Jr., had a grand reunion, and Old Toby joined them to raise his mug of ale in a toast to liberty. Paul was eager to hear the story of the cannon trek, and Will soon had a wide-eyed mob around him as he relived the great adventure.

The Boston victory—like a stone thrown into a pond—spread wide ripples across the cities and towns of America.

Everyone knew that there were years of danger and struggle ahead. The battle wouldn't be an easy one. But the triumph in Boston put new life into the young nation. It proved to the colonists that they could indeed defy mighty England and win.

Colonel Knox, of course, was the hero of the hour, praised and congratulated by all. But, as he pointed out to Lucy, he was too busy to take much notice. He had a thousand things to do, and one of them was to hand in an exact list of his expenses during the long trip. Henry's final bill to the congress, for hiring drivers, horses and oxen, buying rope, tackle, animal forage, and so on, was 520 pounds, 15 shillings, and 8½ pence.

So, in colonial money of that period, the journey cost about $2,500—a real bargain considering that it may very well have saved the American Revolution.

# Other Reading

Would you like to read more about America's War for Independence and the people who served in it? If so, here are other books that may be of special interest:

Boatner, Mark M. *Encyclopedia of the American Revolution.* New York: David M. McKay, 1966.

Callahan, North. *Henry Knox, General Washington's General.* New York: Rinehart, 1958.

Chidsey, Donald Barr. *The Siege of Boston: An On-the-Scene Account of the Beginning of the American Revolution.* New York: Crown Publishers, 1966.

Evans, R. E. *The War of American Independence.* England: Cambridge University Press, 1987.

Forbes, Esther. *Paul Revere and the World He Lived In.* Boston: Houghton Mifflin, 1942.

Knight, James E. *Salem Days*. New Jersey: Troll Associates, 1982.

Montross, Lynn. *Rag, Tag and Bobtail: The Story of the Continental Army*. New York: Harper & Bros., 1952.

Scheer, G. F., and Rankin, H. F. *Rebels and Redcoats*. New York: World Publishing, 1972.